THE COLOSIMO TRIAL

A Novel

By William Eleazer

The Colosimo Trial — Copyright © 2019

By William Eleazer

All rights reserved. No part of this publication (except for brief quotations in articles or reviews) may be reproduced, stored in a retrieval system, or transmitted in any form or by any means, electronic, mechanical, photocopying, recording, or otherwise, without authorization by the publisher.

ISBN – 978-0-578-60535-7 (paperback)
Library of Congress Control Number: 2019918473

Published by
William Eleazer
5 Crescent Place South
St. Petersburg, Florida 33711
wreleazer@gmail.com

Book cover and interior formatting by ebookpbook.
Website: https://www.ebookpbook.com

Printed in the United States of America

First Edition

DEDICATION

As with my first three novels, *Savannah Law*, *The Indictments*, and *The Two-Witness Rule*, this novel—**The Colosimo Trial**—is dedicated to the citizens of Savannah, the beautiful city that has inspired so many artists and writers.

ACKNOWLEDGMENTS

My special thanks to Raechelle Wilson for accepting the task of editing this novel, which required a special talent—as well as bravery and a sense of duty! I also wish to thank Jill Whitworth for assisting with editing. However, should the reader find errors, they remain the sole responsibility of the author.

OTHER NOVELS BY
WILLIAM ELEAZER

Savannah Law, **2010 Gold Medal Winner for Adult Fiction, awarded by the Florida Publishers Association.** A young professor's obsession with a female student at Savannah College of Law takes a surprising turn after Max Gordon, one of the nation's most successful criminal defense attorneys, arrives in Savannah for a high-profile trial. This is a novel about the law, jury trials, lawyers, law schools, and law students. If you love Savannah, the city, you will love *Savannah Law*, the novel.

The Indictments, © **2012.** A brazen robbery by a masked man at one of Savannah's finest restaurants results in the murder of a teenage girl and murder indictments against two defendants. The assistant DA assigned to the case believes one indictment is without merit, and his attempt to have it dismissed threatens both his career and his life. *The Indictments* is a sequel to *Savannah Law* and brings back Scott Marino, the young assistant DA, to once more face ace defense attorney Max Gordon in a Chatham County courtroom. With beautiful Savannah as the locale, this legal thriller will give you many hours of enjoyable and exciting reading.

The Two-Witness Rule, © **2015.** Assistant DA Scott Marino has been assigned a tough case—the prosecution of Max Gordon, one of the nation's most prominent attorneys, accused of paying witnesses to commit perjury in a Savannah criminal trial. Some crimes are just different. One witness is legally sufficient to prove most crimes, even murder—however, for perjury, the "two-witness rule" applies. But Marino is challenged by more than this unique rule. He must prosecute a cunning lawyer defended by another just as crafty. The stakes are high, and he faces threats to his integrity and his life as he prepares for the biggest trial of his young career. The *Two-Witness Rule* is a sequel to *The Indictments* and shares the same locale: beautiful and quaint Savannah, Georgia.

CHAPTER ONE
Tuesday, February 10, 2009

Jennifer Stone sat alone at a small table on the patio outside the Savannah College of Law bookstore. It was a typical February morning in Savannah, chilly at sunrise but turning warm as the day progressed. Jennifer, a senior in her last semester, was nursing a cup of coffee, just killing some time before her eleven o'clock Elder Law class. Her mind wasn't into today's subject, intestate succession. She had more important personal matters on her mind.

Scott Marino, her fiancé, who was an assistant DA in the local DA's office, had called earlier that morning, telling her to make sure she read the local section of today's *South Georgia Times*. She was not a subscriber but purchased a copy as soon as she arrived at the bookstore, and it now lay folded on the table beside her. She had read the article that Scott had called about and quickly realized it could affect their lives. She just wasn't sure exactly how or when.

As she sat gazing out on the busy campus, quietly contemplating the contents of the *Times* article, she heard a voice behind her. It was a familiar voice, but one she had not heard in many months. She turned to find Jessica Valdez, a former classmate, standing a few feet behind her. Jennifer and Jessica were not close friends, but they had taken a class together, and Jennifer knew that Jessica had been a student intern in the DA's office and that Scott had been her supervisor.

What Jennifer did not know was that Scott was also responsible for Jessica being a *former* student. Jessica had sought Scott's assistance with her Advanced Research Project (ARP), a requirement for graduation from Savannah College of Law. Such papers were required to be supervised and signed by a full-time or an adjunct professor, and Scott, as an intern supervisor in the DA's office, was considered an adjunct. When Jessica asked Scott to sign off on her ARP paper, he learned that the paper was, in fact, the work of a law student at another university, and he refused. Then, upon finding that she had submitted the plagiarized paper anyway, he reported it to the law school, resulting in an investigation and her eventual expulsion. It was something he was uncomfortable in doing, but he believed it to be the right thing. He had never shared these events with Jennifer, but Jessica was fully aware of who had reported her plagiarism.

Jennifer turned to face her visitor. "Hi, Jessica! What a nice surprise."

"And nice to see you again, Jennifer. Mind if I join you?"

"No, of course. Sit down. It's been a while; we need to catch up."

Jennifer moved her backpack from the center of the small table, and Jessica took a seat directly across from her.

"Where've you been these past months?" Jennifer asked.

"Atlanta. Working in real estate with my dad's sister. She's a broker, mostly business property. I'm just working as her assistant, learning the ropes."

"So, what brings you back to Savannah?"

"Just stopping by the registrar's office to pick up my grade transcript. Thought I might have a problem, considering the circumstances of my departure. So rather than write, I decided on a personal visit. But it was easy. Took only a few minutes to get a copy, so I have a few hours to kill before my plane."

Jennifer did not know anything about the "circumstances of her departure," but the words put up a warning sign. She was curious but decided not to inquire.

"You're applying to another law school?"

"Yes, there are a couple of night law schools in Atlanta. I can keep working in real estate while attending. I'm really looking forward to completing my degree. It would be really helpful if I stay in real estate. So that's where I am. How about you? Still seeing Scott?"

"A bit more than that. Scott and I are getting married next month."

Jessica paused before replying. It was a long pause. Finally, "When is the big event?"

"March twenty-first. That's the Saturday before our spring break. It will be a very small wedding as far as Savannah weddings go. Scott has few relatives, and I'm an only child. Left my hometown in Missouri when my parents retired and moved to Hilton Head. That was almost seven years ago, right after high school. Haven't been back but once since, so I've lost contact with most of my old high school friends. Neither of my parents has any close relatives. So, relatives in attendance will be few. My mom and dad, Scott's mom—a widow—and his only sister from Tennessee and maybe a cousin from Augusta. That's it. But that's OK. Scott and I have lots of local friends who'll help us celebrate—at last count the total was eighty-two, mostly friends and classmates from Savannah Law."

These last words—"friends and classmates from Savannah Law"—made Jennifer pause. She was speaking to an *uninvited* friend and classmate. Though not a close friend, still a classmate, one who had also been an intern supervised by Scott in the DA's office. It was somewhat of an awkward moment. She made a quick decision.

"And Jessica, we would love for you to attend. I'm sure you would know many others who'll be there. I've asked Nicole—Nicole Chapman—to be my maid of honor. You know her. She'll be my only attendant. And you remember Sue Draper, from our Federal Courts Seminar. And Joy White, too. We're sending electronic invitations, so I just need your email address. Here, write it down for me." Jennifer reached in her backpack and removed a small notepad and pen.

"I'm excited for you," said Jessica. "And I haven't even said 'congratulations!' You know I would love to attend. If you have time now, let me hear all about it." Jessica wrote down her email address and handed the notepad back to Jennifer.

But she had no intention of attending this wedding. She had had her eyes on Scott from the time she met him at the DA's office—thrown herself at him would be more precise. And he had rejected her advances and informed on her. She held him personally responsible for her working in Atlanta as a flunky for her aunt in real estate, rather than continuing at Savannah Law and looking forward to a JD degree in May. Her dismissal was a very embarrassing time for her and equally embarrassing for her father, a prominent Miami attorney. Jessica, characteristically, denied the plagiarism to her father, and characteristically, he believed her. He promptly filed a lawsuit and had one of his office investigators look into it. The investigator quickly determined the plagiarism claim was indeed true and the lawsuit was withdrawn almost as soon as it commenced. The wonderful relationship Jessica enjoyed with her father was seriously wounded. She was living at home, but they were barely speaking to each other. Jessica could see the hurt in her father every day, and the offer from her aunt in Atlanta to join her real estate office was quickly accepted.

Jennifer was pleased that Jessica had asked for details of the wedding. This was the most exciting time of her life, and she enjoyed sharing it. "Well, as I mentioned, it will be a small wedding. My mom who lives in Hilton Head with my dad is doing most of the planning—and my dad is doing all of the paying. We need both kinds of help. The planning is going smoothly. Of all the decisions that have been made, Mom and I had a different idea on only one. That was who should preside over the ceremony. Mom wanted her pastor from Hilton Head to do the honors. I wanted Roger Bacon, assistant pastor at Bonaventure Community Church, which I attend often, to preside. Roger's wife Lisa is one of my good friends from SCAD. I won that one." Jennifer smiled and took a sip from her coffee before continuing.

"The wedding ceremony will be at five with dinner and dancing following—all out at the Winery on Wilmington Island. It's a beautiful pavilion, and I think it's a perfect site for a wedding, rain or shine."

"I agree," said Jessica. "I've seen it. Beautiful view of the marshes, especially at sunset."

"And surprisingly inexpensive to rent for the day," said Jennifer. "Scott and I made a firm decision to limit the expenses. Neither of us is from a wealthy family, and law school tuition has been expense enough. With just a maid of honor and a best man, no rehearsal needed and no rehearsal dinner. And I didn't even have to buy a wedding gown. My mother has saved hers all these years, and with just a little alteration, it fits me perfectly. It's a silver-white crepe sheath, floor-length. I love it. So, we are keeping the expenses down, but we'll still have a nice little wedding at the Winery. Catered by Sybil and Sons—they offered a good food selection at a reasonable price. We'll have several big-name bands." Jennifer grinned. "Well, big bands on CDs, presided over by Juri. You remember Juri, from the Library, don't you?"

The "Library" was a bar and restaurant located adjacent to Savannah College of Law. Almost all the students were acquainted with it and its management, which included Juri. The Library was a large granite-faced building, built in the 1920s as a county public library, but converted into a bar and restaurant about the time the law school opened. Juri's older brother, Jaak, was the owner and Juri was his main assistant and head bartender. Their unusual first names reflected their Estonian heritage. Their mother and father emigrated from Estonia to the United States shortly after World War II and settled in Springfield, a small town near Savannah.

"Of course," responded Jessica. "How can you forget Juri, disc jockey *and* bartender? I recall he had a massive collection of records of all musical styles. That should be fun. After the party, a honeymoon to where?"

"We're staying close. Just a few days at The Lodge on St. Simons Island. Scott is carrying a big load at the DA's office. They are

shorthanded right now, several unexpected departures recently—
and he hopes to get a crack at a case the grand jury just handed down
involving a prominent attorney from Atlanta."

"My new home town. An attorney—how is he involved?"

"As the defendant," said Jennifer. "It's in today's *South Georgia
Times*. Here, I have a copy." Jennifer reached for the folded paper,
found the article and handed the paper to Jessica, noting with her
finger the short article reporting the results of the Chatham County
Grand Jury.

Jessica took the paper and began to read it silently. It was a short
article but with a large-type headline placed prominently on the first
page of the "local news" section.

PROMINENT ATLANTA ATTORNEY INDICTED

James A. Colosimo and two employees of his Atlanta law firm,
Anderson H. McDowell and Thomas J. Reid, were indicted by a
Chatham County grand jury yesterday. Each was charged with in-
fluencing witnesses and conspiracy to influence witnesses.

Mr. Colosimo, who prefers to be known as "Diamond Jim"
Colosimo, had represented Chicago attorney Maxwell Gordon
in a highly publicized trial in Savannah last November. Gordon
was found not guilty after a jury trial but was killed shortly afterward in a confrontation with Clarence Wilborn just outside
the courthouse entrance. Wilborn, an attorney from Macon, had
once served as co-counsel with Gordon in a criminal trial and had
testified as a prosecution witness against Gordon at the trial in
November. Apparently upset by the not guilty verdict, Wilburn
confronted Gordon and held him at gunpoint near the "Flame
of Freedom" monument at the entrance to the courthouse. In a
scene shown live on TV, Wilburn fatally shot Gordon. Almost si-
multaneously, Wilborn was fatally shot by a member of the Metro
Police SWAT team, which had been called to the scene as it was
unfolding.

A spokesman for the Chatham County District Attorney's Office reported that each of the three men indicted will be arraigned on February 12. It is unknown if any of the three have retained counsel.

Jessica handed the newspaper back to Jennifer. "Scott wants to get involved in that new case?" she asked, quickly adding, "Was he involved in the Gordon trial?" It was a question, but she already knew the answer. She had followed the trial closely. The trial and the shooting afterward were reported in the Atlanta newspapers and on Atlanta TV, and she had viewed most of it. She was quite aware of Scott's participation but did not want to reveal any knowledge or special interest.

"Yes, he prosecuted the Gordon case. And lost," said Jennifer. "I would think he would want out of this one, but he wants in. And he says he thinks he'll be assigned the case because he knows more about the facts surrounding it than anyone in the office." Jennifer looked at her watch.

"Better head for class. I'll send the wedding invitation to your email address this afternoon. It'll have all the details. I'm using Evite. It's a great program for sending invitations. And everyone invited can learn who's attending. Helps with ride-sharing. Makes planning easier for everyone."

Jennifer stood and picked up her backpack. "Really glad to see you again, Jessica. And I'm so glad you can come to the wedding. You'll see a lot of your old classmates. Hope you have a nice flight back to Atlanta."

"Thanks," replied Jessica as she stood and smiled at Jennifer. "I look forward to seeing you and Scott on your big day."

"Still got a lot of planning to do, but it's exciting and fun," said Jennifer as she placed her backpack over her shoulder and walked away.

Jessica was still smiling. She had some plans of her own.

CHAPTER TWO

February 9

Jessica began to make her plans as soon as Jennifer left. It had all occurred to her as she was reading the news article. She wasn't at all sure she could pull it off, but it was worth trying. She sat down at the table, removed a small pad from her pocketbook, and began to make notes. She wanted to record a few things she had just learned while it was fresh on her mind. First, "Sybil and Sons," the caterer. The Lodge at St. Simons. And presiding, Roger Bacon of Bonaventure Community Church. Then she noted the names that Jennifer had mentioned who would be attending—Nicole Chapman, Sue Draper, Joy White. She would get the rest of the names from the Evite invitation Jennifer would be sending. She was familiar with Evite invitation software, having received a couple of Evite invitations during the past year. Someone inviting guests with Evite could decide whether to make the RSVP list available to all who receive invitations or limit the viewing to the host. She recalled that Jennifer had indicated that she had sent the invitations so that all guests would be able to view the RSVP list. Getting the names of wedding guests would not take much effort. However, it would take a while to get all the phone numbers, but it could be done, even if she had to spend a few dollars on websites that do that sort of work.

She had a couple of hours before she had to be at the airport to catch her plane back to Atlanta. She had her laptop with her, so she drove in her rental car to Oglethorpe Mall where, she recalled, free Wi-Fi was available. There were several restaurants in the mall where she could have lunch and then spend some time catching up with friends on Facebook.

The restaurant she chose was not crowded, and she found a table in the quietest part. She ordered a salad, service was quick, and soon she was on her laptop viewing the latest news from her friends. About an hour later, she received an email. It was from Jennifer. It was the invitation, and it had a block to click for her RSVP—yes, no, and maybe. And just as Jennifer had promised, the entire RSVP list was there for viewing. Jessica smiled at the extensive list of names on her laptop. *This is going even easier than expected; just have to connect the names to phone numbers.*

She had one more task before returning to Atlanta—she needed to purchase another cell phone. She already had the latest Apple iPhone, but it would not be appropriate for use with her plan. She wanted one with a number not traceable back to her in any way. A new phone, with Savannah's 912 area code, would be ideal. For the curious, that would indicate any calls she made from that phone originated from Savannah.

After leaving the restaurant, she checked the mall directory and found there was a cell phone store near the parking lot entrance. She didn't need a monthly plan, just one for which she could purchase air time. She found a very basic phone that she liked and received a number with a 912 area code. She gave her name as "Celen Domingo." On a whim, she gave her address as 422 Mentirosa St., Savannah. "Mentirosa" in Spanish translates to "liar." She was sure the young blond geek processing her purchase was unaware of the meaning or the fact that no such street existed in Savannah. It struck her as funny, and she smiled as she paid cash for the phone and twenty-five hours of air time—which was much more air time than she ever expected to use with this phone.

The return to Atlanta was uneventful. She felt good about her new phone—and her plan for its eventual use.

CHAPTER THREE

Tuesday, February 10

Jennifer arrived at the front steps to the Library Bar and Grill at 5:30 p.m. She had been involved in research for a class project for most of the afternoon at the Savannah College of Law Library, just a block away. She was to meet Scott at the Library Bar after he got off work. Her timing was perfect; Scott was pulling into the adjacent parking lot just as she arrived. After Scott parked and gave her a quick kiss, they walked up the steps and through the heavy oak doors of the Library entrance. It was a Tuesday, and the evening crowd had not begun to arrive. The tables in the large room were mostly empty. They noted Juri on duty behind the bar, serving a couple at the far end. They took seats at the center of the bar. As soon as Juri saw them, he smiled and walked toward them.

"Hi, Jennifer . . . Scott. My favorite bride and groom-to-be. But you haven't been in for a while. Where 'ya been?"

"Juri, both of us were here last Friday. I have to put in some hours at work to earn enough money to pay for your overpriced drinks, and Jennifer prefers to avoid you because of your 'blonde' jokes. Be happy we're here again," replied Scott.

"I am. And speaking of jokes, I've got a good story for you. Are you ready?" Juri never called his jokes "jokes"—they were always a "story."

"Does it make any difference if we are ready?" replied Jennifer.

"Nope. But where are my manners? I haven't even taken your orders."

"House chardonnay for me," said Jennifer.

"And a draft beer for me, Juri—an IPA, if you have some that you haven't watered down too much," said Scott.

Juri served Jennifer's chardonnay and then filled a frosted mug with Scott's IPA. And as was his custom, he slid the mug ten feet down the bar top with just the amount of force to stop it right where Scott was seated. "Perfect! And just the right amount of water added. I know you complain, Scott, but adding water helps me keep my prices low. I'm customer-oriented. And now for that story. Sorry to disappoint, Jennifer, not a blonde joke. This one I've been saving for Scott." Juri was already smiling as he began.

"Son goes in and tells his dad, 'I want to get married.'"

"Dad says, 'Are you sure you're ready?'"

"Son replies, 'I'm sure.'"

"Dad says, 'Well tell me you're sorry.'"

"Son looks puzzled. 'Sorry for what?'"

"Dad says, 'Say sorry.'"

"Son says, 'But for what? What did I do?'"

"Dad says, 'Just say sorry.'"

"Son says, 'But . . . what have I done wrong?'"

"Dad says, 'Say sorry.'"

Juri started laughing, turning his head from Scott to Jennifer and back, making sure he had their close attention. He stopped laughing, but the smile remained.

"Son says, 'Please, just tell me why?'"

"Dad: 'Say sorry.'"

"Son: 'OK, Dad . . . I'm sorry.'"

"Dad says, 'There! You've finished your training. You've got it! When you learn to say "sorry" for no reason at all, then you're ready to get married!'"

Juri started laughing again, turning to Scott, then to Jennifer, and back again, looking for their approval. Both laughed briefly, smiling at Juri, who, of course, was enjoying his joke more than either of them.

Then Scott managed a deliberate scowl. "That was awful, Juri. Beyond awful."

Jennifer offered her critique pumping both fists, thumbs down, yet still smiling. But that was the way it usually went—Juri's hearty laughter drowning out any vocal disapproval and ignoring any disapproving gestures.

"Yes, that was bad, Juri, as usual, but at least it wasn't another blonde joke," said Jennifer.

"That one was for Scott. Here's one for you . . ."

Scott interrupted and held a palm out to Juri. "No mas, no mas, Juri, but thanks for the marriage lesson. Sorry, Jennifer, sorry—see, I'm a fast learner." Scott picked up his beer and Jennifer's wine glass. "Jennifer and I have some important matters to discuss over dinner. Just add the drinks to my tab. We're going next door where it's nice and quiet, and they don't water down the beer."

By "next door" Scott meant the adjacent restaurant, the "grill" part of the Library Bar and Grill. It was separated from the bar area by a glass wall and glass door and was indeed nice and quiet. They took a table in a corner in the far end, their usual spot when they had dinner there, which recently had become weekly.

After they had placed their order, Jennifer was ready to hear more about the indictment noted in the morning paper. "Are you going to be prosecuting 'Diamond Jim' and his crew?"

"Yep, Joe knew I was already acquainted with the facts and the players." Scott was referring to his boss, Joe Fasi, Felony Chief in the DA's office who assigned the felony cases. "But he also gave me the opportunity to turn it down. Said he knew I had a pretty heavy load. But so does everyone else in the office. I told him I was fine with it and would let him know if I needed help. Fact is, I'm really looking forward to trying that case. Seeing 'Diamond Jim' Colosimo sitting in Courtroom K as a defendant and not as a defense counsel should be special."

"I know that Colosimo was the defense counsel in the Max Gordon case last November, but I don't know anything about the other two who were indicted with him. What's their connection?" asked Jennifer.

"McDowell and Reid. Those two work in his office. Reid was once an attorney but was disbarred. Not sure exactly why. McDowell was never an attorney but did graduate from law school. Was never admitted to any bar. Maybe he couldn't pass the bar exam, or maybe he didn't get past the character test. But Colosimo hired him, so I expect it was because he couldn't pass the character test. Colosimo would find that a plus. McDowell and Reid are the ones who actually came to Savannah to try to get our witness, Vijay Patel, to back out of the pretrial agreement he had signed. They visited him late one night when he was alone at his convenience store. Told him we couldn't prove the case because of the two-witness rule. Said his attorney should have told him that, so his attorney was either incompetent or was working with the prosecutor. Suggested that he not mention their visit or this new information to his attorney because after all, his attorney is the one who advised him to sign the pretrial agreement and plead guilty."

"What's Colosimo's involvement?" asked Jennifer.

"They were his agents. They worked for him. He's the one behind the visit—they didn't just drive down to Savannah from Atlanta on their own initiative."

"You and I can be sure of that, but will a jury be so sure?"

"True, juries can surprise you, but there's one other piece of evidence. You've heard me mention Carl DeBickero, the GBI agent who helped with the last trial, haven't you?"

"Many times."

"Well, Carl was the agent who arrested Reid. He gave him a Miranda warning and then began to question him. He asked what Reid was doing in Savannah on the night of October 5—that's the night he visited Patel at the convenience store. Reid replied, 'I go to cities where we have trials pending. I sometimes interview witnesses, take statements, and do whatever is necessary to get the case ready for trial for my boss.' Of course, he does. And getting Patel to not testify was how he was getting the case ready for trial. The conspiracy began with Colosimo and was consummated by Reid and McDowell. All three are guilty of both the conspiracy and the completed crime. And I think I can prove it."

"And I bet you will," said Jennifer. She was smiling. "Any word on who he'll bring in as his defense counsel? I wonder if he'll give Samarkos a call. Wasn't he Max Gordon's attorney before Colosimo got involved?"

"He was. Would be a smart move, but I suspect he'll bring in someone from Atlanta. Reid and McDowell will need attorneys too."

"Perhaps they'll share Colosimo's attorney," said Jennifer.

"No way. That would be a conflict of interest," said Scott.

"Yeah, forgot about that. And before I forget something else, I ran into an old friend at the bookstore today—I should say a mutual friend. Jessica Valdez."

Scott moved back in his chair, a surprised look on his face. "Is she back in school?"

"No, she was on campus to visit the registrar. Picking up her transcript. She's living in Atlanta, working for her aunt in real estate. She wants to finish law school at one of the night law schools in Atlanta. She asked if I was still seeing you, and when I told her we were getting married next month, she wanted to know all about it. And when I told her it was going to be a small wedding, with just family and mostly classmates, I realized she was also a classmate and your former intern—and she had not been invited. So, on the spur of the moment, I invited her and she accepted. And yes, I know we had agreed to keep the guest list small, but I was sure you would approve. You do, don't you?"

Scott hoped his facial expression did not reveal the answer he wanted to give. But he loved this woman. She could invite anyone she wished and he would approve. He wanted to say, *No, no, Jennifer. Not Jessica Valdez! Please tell me you are joking!*

Scott considered telling Jennifer about the plagiarism and his involvement in her expulsion from Savannah Law. This would be an opportune moment. He paused for a few seconds before replying. If he told Jennifer about the plagiarism, what good would it do? The invitation was already made and accepted.

So, he gave his answer. "Of course. Good decision. It's still a small wedding as Savannah weddings go." Then he changed the subject to some planning that was still pending for the wedding. But the thought of Jessica Valdez attending their wedding was still on his mind.

CHAPTER FOUR

Friday, February 13

It was a few minutes after 9:00 a.m. when Superior Court Judge Gail Feather called the first case on Friday's arraignment docket: "James A. Colosimo. Anderson H. McDowell. Thomas J. Reid."

The three named defendants were seated in the first row of the courtroom. They quickly rose, walked to the front of the courtroom and stopped about ten feet in front of the judge's bench. Colosimo— "Diamond Jim"—was in the middle with Reid on his right and McDowell on his left. Scott had wondered if Colosimo would show up in his garish "Diamond Jim" outfit. And of course, he did. Wearing his white linen suit, with diamonds adorning his fingers, wristwatch, cufflinks, and necktie, he was a striking and to most observers, Scott was sure, a bizarre figure to be standing as a defendant in a Chatham County courtroom. His black mustache covered his upper lip and a substantial portion of both sides of his face, matching the image of the original "Diamond Jim" hanging near the entrance of his restaurant in Atlanta. His fingernails were the only change in appearance that Scott noted. They were sparkling in a white diamond gloss. And something else he had missed at the previous trial: the length of the nails on the little finger of each hand. They extended at least three-quarters of an inch beyond the flesh. It reminded Scott of his high school algebra teacher who kept one little fingernail at a similar length. When the class seemed to be losing attention, he would scrape the fingernail across the blackboard, and the class would immediately snap to attention. He smiled as he thought of "Diamond Jim" using this technique on an inattentive jury.

Scott was alone at the prosecution table. He was the assigned lead counsel for the prosecution but would be assisted by Joe Fasi, Felony Chief, during the trial. This was a high-profile case, and while Fasi had complete confidence in Scott's trial skills, Scott was not one of the experienced prosecutors to whom such cases were usually assigned. Fasi would serve as second chair, but the prosecution case would be presented entirely by Scott. They had teamed this way in previous trials, with Fasi conducting the jury selection and Scott handling the rest.

Scott stood and looked around the courtroom to see who would be coming forward as defense counsel for the trio. The courtroom had a couple of dozen people in the front rows. Several were local defense attorneys, but none moved. No local attorneys had contacted Scott about the case, and no attorney had filed a notice of representation for any of the defendants. Scott saw no one rising from the benches. He did see a familiar face—Bill Baldwin, a reporter for the *South Georgia Times*, who had covered the Max Gordon trial and several previous trials that Scott had prosecuted. He was not surprised that Baldwin was present, and he expected him to call later with a multitude of questions. He always did.

Judge Feather waited a few moments and also gazed around the courtroom. Then she addressed the three men in front of her. "Do any of you have representation?"

Both McDowell and Reid turned to Colosimo, who replied, "Yes, we each have an attorney."

Scott noticed that Colosimo did not address the judge with "Your Honor," as attorneys usually do when addressing a judge in court. But it was what Scott had come to expect. Not once during the Max Gordon trial in which Colosimo served as defense attorney, did Colosimo use the salutation, "Your Honor." It was obviously a deliberate choice, and apparently, he would continue to avoid this traditional courtesy. Scott was at a loss to see any advantage in this odd conduct, but odd conduct seemed to be a signature trait of this Atlanta attorney.

"Were you expecting your attorneys to be here this morning?" asked Judge Feather.

"Yes, and our attorney is present," replied Colosimo. "I, James Colosimo, will be representing the three defendants in this case. Each of us pleads not guilty. We understand the charges are influencing witnesses and conspiracy to influence witnesses. We waive reading of the indictments. Each of us has a copy. We request trial by jury and ask for ten days to file motions."

Judge Feather shifted in her chair to a more upright posture. Her face showed a look of astonishment, and she waited a long moment before speaking.

"You are saying that you will be self-represented and will also be representing Mr. McDowell and Mr. Reid?"

"Correct," responded Colosimo, continuing to omit the customary "Your Honor."

Scott was as astonished by this as the judge. "Shocked" would be more accurate. He had never even considered such a scenario. He was sure there was such a conflict of interest that it would be malpractice. He was confident that Judge Feather would not permit such representation. But he had other concerns. He had expected to offer either Reid or McDowell—or perhaps both—a pretrial agreement for testifying for the prosecution in the case. The real bad actor was, of course, Colosimo who initiated and directed the crimes. Neither of his associates would have traveled from Atlanta to Savannah to contact a potential witness in the Gordon case without directions from Colosimo. It was Colosimo who should receive the most severe punishment and eventual disbarment. Now, should Colosimo be permitted to represent himself as well as Reid and McDowell, Scott could not contact either of Colosimo's associates. If he offered a pretrial it would have to go through their attorney—Colosimo. Fat chance, he knew.

Judge Feather looked sternly at the three men standing before her, then focused her eyes on Colosimo. "Mr. Colosimo," she began, "such representation would be highly irregular with multiple conflicts of interest. Rule 1.7 of the Bar Rules covers your situation in detail and outlines why such representations would be impermissible. Each of you is entitled to an attorney who will give total loyalty. As noted in the rule, loyalty and independent judgment are essential elements in a lawyer's relationship to a client. There is simply too much potential for conflict to allow the multiple representations that you propose. In fact, I am even concerned that you wish to represent yourself. These are serious felony charges. You should seek counsel to assist your own defense."

"Your concern is of no importance to me," Colosimo responded. "I am entitled to represent myself. Even if I were not a highly successful and experienced attorney—which I am—I would be entitled to self-representation. Perhaps you are not familiar with the Faretta case from the United States Supreme Court. I have a copy in my briefcase—would you like me to get it for you?" The tone as well as the words were insulting, which seemed to be exactly what Colosimo intended.

Judge Feather looked at the bailiff with a suppressed smile. She had every right to demand a respectful tone from attorneys in her court, but she had a full docket for the morning and would not be drawn into a confrontation. She would proceed.

"That will not be necessary, Mr. Colosimo. I am aware you are a member of the Georgia Bar. I am not aware of how successful or experienced you claim to be, but in view of your bar membership, the holding in Faretta, and your desire to represent yourself, I have no authority to preclude you from doing so, as foolish as I believe that to be. So, let's turn our attention to whether you may represent Mr. Reid and Mr. McDowell. Let me discuss the matter first with Mr. McDowell."

Judge Feather turned and faced Anderson McDowell. McDowell was in his early thirties, just a bit under six feet tall. With a wiry body, he had a long slender face with an extended forehead. He parted his light brown hair in the middle and wore thick sideburns down to his chin, which did not improve his rather plain appearance.

"I want you to understand, Mr. McDowell, that you are entitled to counsel of your own choice, someone who will give you his or her utmost loyalty and independent judgment. You and Mr. Colosimo are charged with the same crime, but it is quite possible that your interest and the interest of Mr. Colosimo are not the same. Even if it appears now that they are, as the trial proceeds you may discover that they are not the same. Has Mr. Colosimo discussed such possible conflict with you?"

"We have had lengthy discussions about this, Your Honor. Our defenses are joined—they are the same. I believe there could be no conflict."

"What is your relationship to Mr. Colosimo?"

"I am employed by him. I work in his office as a paralegal and investigator."

"What is your education?"

"I have a business degree from college as well as a JD degree," replied McDowell.

Judge Feather paused for a long moment. "A JD degree? Are you a member of any state bar?"

"No, Your Honor. I have not ever been admitted to any state bar."

Scott was surprised at the personal appearance of Anderson McDowell. He looked so much younger than the photo he had seen on Colosimo's website. Scott wondered if the website photo had been manipulated to make him appear "more mature." Today in court, he appeared to be in his late twenties or early thirties and Reid close to forty.

"Let me ask these questions now to Mr. Reid." She turned and looked at the defendant on the right of Colosimo. Reid was a few inches taller than McDowell and appeared several years older. He had dark brown hair that he wore rather short, and unlike McDowell, he parted it on the side. With gold frameless glasses and an expensive pin-striped suit, he looked like a veteran courtroom attorney.

"Did you hear me explain to Mr. McDowell that you are entitled to counsel of your own choice, someone who will give you complete loyalty and independent judgment?"

"Yes, I did."

"And you understand that both you and Mr. Colosimo are charged with the same crimes and that even though you may believe you share the same defense or defenses without conflict, as the trial proceeds his interest and yours may not remain the same. Have you discussed your defenses with Mr. Colosimo as well as any possible conflicts?"

"We have discussed all of that at length. And just as Mr. McDowell said, our defenses are one and the same, and we believe it best to have a joint and unified defense under the direction of Mr. Colosimo, our attorney. My research of the law leads me to believe that I am entitled to have an attorney of my own choice. Both the Sixth Amendment to the United States Constitution and Paragraph Fourteen of our Georgia Constitution's Bill of Rights guarantees me that right. And I am exercising my right to have Mr. Colosimo as my attorney."

"What is your education, Mr. Reid?" asked Judge Feather.

"I have an undergraduate degree in Political Science and a JD degree from Clarence Darrow Law School in Nashville. It's a small night law school."

"Are you a member of any state bar?"

"I was once a member of the Tennessee Bar. I am no longer."

Judge Feather paused, a frown on her face, but she did not ask why he was no longer a member of the Tennessee Bar. Scott was disappointed; he was very curious about the reason for his disbarment.

"What is your relationship with Mr. Colosimo?"

"Well, like Andy," he gestured with his thumb toward Anderson McDowell on the other side of Colosimo, "I'm employed as a paralegal and investigator."

Scott noted that Reid, unlike McDowell, followed his boss's lead in omitting "Your Honor" when addressing the court. He reasoned this was because Reid was the older of the two and likely had been working for Colosimo longer, picking up his habits—perhaps under instructions or just instinctively following his lead.

"I have a number of concerns about allowing the representation of you two by Mr. Colosimo. There are practical considerations as well as ethical considerations. It may occur that during the course of proceedings in this case that not only may Mr. Colosimo's interest diverge from the interests of one of his clients, but the interests of his clients may also differ from each other, making it impossible for Mr. Colosimo to give loyalty and independent advice to both." She paused and sat back in her chair, appearing to be in deep thought.

Scott stood at the prosecution table, and Judge Feather turned to look at him. "May I be heard, Your Honor?"

"Yes, Mr. Marino."

Scott had his laptop with him at the table, and as soon as Judge Feather had mentioned Rule 1.7 of the Bar Rules, he had pulled up the rules on his computer. During the discussion that Judge Feather was having with Colosimo and his two associates, he had been reading the rules.

"Your Honor, paragraph 5 of the comments to Rule 1.7 appears to be particularly pertinent to the request by Mr. Colosimo. It reads, 'A client may give informed consent to representation notwithstanding a conflict. However, when a disinterested lawyer would conclude that the client should not agree to the representation under the circumstances, the lawyer involved cannot properly ask for such agreement or provide representation on the basis of the client's informed consent.' Your Honor, I submit that no disinterested lawyer could conclude that Mr. Reid or Mr. McDowell should consent to the representation as proposed by Mr. Colosimo. Such representation should not be permitted."

Colosimo turned and looked sternly at Scott. "Now isn't this special," he said. "The prosecutor in a criminal case giving advice to the judge as to who should be the defense counsel in the case. I'm sure the appellate courts will find this new procedure fascinating. Perhaps the bar rules will be amended, requiring that all defendants get the prosecutor's approval of their selected attorney. Yes, the prosecutor's approval—and make that at least ten days before trial. Or perhaps require a selection from a list of defense attorneys approved by the district attorney. But until that day comes, these two men are entitled to an attorney of their own choice, and they have made their choice."

Scott realized he perhaps deserved the sarcasm and ridicule. Judge Feather was an experienced and intelligent jurist, quite capable of making this decision without his input. She had not asked for his assistance, and she had already indicated her familiarity with Rule 1.7, which included the language he had just read. He regretted getting involved in the conflict discussion, and he chose not to attempt to respond to Colosimo.

The courtroom was stilled for a long moment after Colosimo spoke. Judge Feather was the next to speak. "Mr. Colosimo, have you obtained in writing the informed consent of Mr. Reid and Mr. McDowell in which they note your advice as to risks and alternatives to your representation?"

"Yes. I have signed statements in which each acknowledges that we have discussed the case individually and jointly; have discussed all possible defenses and all possible conflicts; that they are aware that I will be representing both of them as well as myself on identical charges; that they are aware of alternatives including individual defense attorneys of their choosing; and that they waive the potential conflict in this case. I have the papers right here." Colosimo held the papers in his hand as he spoke.

Judge Feather nodded to a bailiff, who took the papers and delivered them to the judge, who began reading them. This was going to be a difficult decision, and she knew of no previous court decisions on the issue. She had had quite a number of defendants request self-representation during her years on the bench. Most dropped the request after she advised them of the danger inherent in self-representation.

Judge Feather paused her reading, looked at the three men standing in front of her, and announced a ten-minute recess. "All rise!" the bailiff called, and Judge Feather departed for her chambers.

As she sat at her desk reading the papers, she reflected on her possible choices. None were appealing. She was sure that what Colosimo and his two associates were seeking was not in the interest of justice nor in the interest of any of the participants—except perhaps Colosimo. She also thought of the California judge in the Faretta case who had an analogous decision to make many years before. Requiring a defendant to be assisted by counsel would have been deemed a safe decision then. In fact, the judge's decision to deny Faretta that right was approved by two appellate courts before certiorari was granted by the U.S. Supreme Court. There it was reversed, finding that the California courts deprived him of his constitutional right to conduct his own defense. This was despite the fact that nothing in the constitutions of California or the United States specifically addresses the right of self-representation. In this case, Judge Feather faced a much different situation. Both the California Constitution and the United States Constitution specifically provide for an accused to have counsel, and that had generally been interpreted to mean any licensed attorney of choice. She had called for only a ten-minute recess and thought of extending the time so she could research the issue. But she had a busy docket; other cases were there for arraignment. This was her case, and it would be her decision. She would announce it in open court in a few minutes.

CHAPTER FIVE
Friday, February 13

Judge Feather entered the courtroom as the bailiff again called "All Rise." She took her seat on the bench and motioned for the spectators to be seated. The three defendants promptly walked forward and stood to face the judge.

"I have read the signed statements and waivers of Mr. Reid and Mr. McDowell," she began. "I have previously advised each of you—Mr. Reid and Mr. McDowell—of the serious danger in choosing the same counsel and the additional danger in view of the fact that your chosen counsel is facing the identical felony charges that you are facing. The guiding principle of any criminal trial is that justice shall be done. And in my opinion, based on years of criminal trial experience both as counsel and as a trial judge, you—as well as justice—would be better served if each of you had individual and separate counsel, not counsel facing the same charges as you. So, I ask you once again, is it still your absolute and personal choice to be represented by Mr. Colosimo?"

"Yes, that is my choice," replied Reid.

McDowell looked down and did not reply. Judge Feather looked directly at him.

"Mr. McDowell?"

McDowell looked up at the judge and waited a long moment before replying. "May I have a few minutes to think about this again, Your Honor?"

"Of course, Mr. McDowell. You take a seat in the courtroom and consider your decision very carefully. Meanwhile, I'll continue with the other arraignments that I have on the calendar for today. Mr. Colosimo and Mr. Reid, you also take a seat in the courtroom. Do not consult with Mr. McDowell unless he approaches you and explicitly requests to speak with you. This is his decision. I'll call this case again later this morning." The three men walked to the spectator section and took seats, Colosimo and Reid near the back of the courtroom and McDowell on a different row closer to the front.

As Judge Feather was about to call the next case, she looked at the first row where the attorneys who were waiting for the call of their cases were seated. She noted Morrie Goldman, an attorney who had recently left a civil trial firm and was now on his own, practicing criminal law. There had been courthouse gossip that he made the move to criminal law after being dismissed from his firm. The dismissal, or any reason for it, was never verified, but it was known that he had engaged Charles Samarkos, an experienced criminal trial attorney, shortly before he left the firm. After he left, he switched his practice to criminal law. Although Goldman had appeared before Judge Feather in a civil case, this was the first time he had appeared before her in his new role.

"I see Mr. Goldman in court today. Welcome, Mr. Goldman. Did you hear my conversation with the young man—Mr. McDowell—a few moments ago?"

Goldman stood to respond. "Yes, Your Honor, I did."

"Would you be willing to answer questions about representation should Mr. McDowell have a question?"

"Of course, Your Honor."

She looked toward McDowell, who was now seated. "Mr. McDowell, standing up front is Mr. Morrie Goldman, an attorney. He is willing to discuss with you any questions you have about representation, should you have any. You are not required to discuss any matter with him, but should you wish to do so, he is willing to answer. And it will all be private and privileged. Do you understand?"

McDowell rose from his seat to reply. "Yes, Your Honor."

"Mr. Goldman, you and Mr. McDowell may be seated. We'll now continue with arraignments."

Scott looked on approvingly. He liked her style. He knew that Goldman had left his civil law firm, and he had heard that Goldman had recently hired an attorney because of some dispute at the firm. Perhaps Judge Feather also knew this, and it is why she had called on Goldman for this unusual consultation. Hopefully, Goldman could convince McDowell that he should seek his own individual counsel.

Scott moved to the end of the prosecution table. The other cases for arraignment that morning involved other assistant DAs, and they could have the table as needed. He would use the time until he was called again, to do some research with his laptop. He still did not know how Judge Feather would rule, but it appeared that she was leaning toward approving the requests. Perhaps there were cases on point that he could find with his computer.

It did not take long. And it was a Supreme Court case, *U.S. v. Wheat*, decided thirteen years after the Faretta case. Scott read it carefully while Judge Feather proceeded with arraignments for two additional cases on her morning docket. Just as Scott had completed reading the twenty-page Supreme Court decision, Judge Feather once again called his case. He watched the three defendants walk forward and stand before the judge's bench. They were in the same positions, Colosimo in the middle. Scott had only a fleeting moment to make his decision: Should he bring the new case to the judge's attention? He recalled the spontaneous rebuke he had received from Colosimo after his earlier comments. He wasn't anxious for more. But assessing Judge Feather's remarks to Reid and McDowell just before McDowell requested some time to think over the matter, it appeared that the judge was going to grant the request. The prosecution of these crimes was going to be difficult enough without this obstacle. He knew he would need the testimony of one of Colosimo's associates for a conviction. With Colosimo as the attorney for both, that option was out.

He decided to wait until he heard from McDowell. If McDowell decided he wanted his own separate attorney and Reid remained in the pact, he would simply negotiate a pretrial with McDowell. Problem solved.

Judge Feather focused her eyes on Anderson McDowell. "Mr. McDowell, have you had the time needed to make your decision?"

"I have, Your Honor. I am aware of the possible conflict, and I stand with my waiver. I want Mr. Colosimo to represent me."

Scott's heart sank. Now he felt compelled to address the court. He would have to act quickly. He rose and took a couple of steps in front of the table where he had been sitting.

"Your Honor. While we were waiting for Mr. McDowell to make his decision, I did some research on my laptop and found a Supreme Court case I would like to call to your attention."

Judge Feather looked at Scott but did not respond immediately. Scott took that as permission to continue. He wasted no time.

"The case is *Wheat v. United States*, found at 386 U.S. 153, a 1988 case. The facts were, of course, different, but the case did involve, as in the present case, two co-defendants charged with a criminal conspiracy who wanted to be represented by the same attorney. And, like the present case, they had signed fully informed waivers of any conflict of interest because of such dual representation."

Scott looked at the notes he had quickly written when he was reading the case, but he did not pause. "The Supreme Court summed up the issue this way: 'To what extent is a criminal defendant's right to his chosen attorney qualified by the fact that the attorney represented other defendants in the same criminal conspiracy?' In answering that question . . ."

Scott checked his notes again and quickly continued. "The court noted that the essential aim of the Sixth Amendment is to guarantee an effective advocate for each criminal defendant rather than to ensure a defendant is represented by the lawyer he prefers. The Supreme Court, like every lower court that examined the case, found that the judge acted properly in refusing the defendants' request for dual representation. I have no recommendation to make regarding this decision, but I believe it appropriate to bring this case to the court's attention as the issue is so similar."

Colosimo's face began to flush as soon as Scott began to speak, and by the time Scott had finished, sweat was forming on his temple, and his neck veins were visibly enlarged. He turned from Scott to Judge Feather.

"Judge," he said, "I've tried cases in magistrate courts, municipal courts, probate courts, juvenile courts, state courts, superior courts, and federal courts. Hundreds of cases—from Valdosta to Chattanooga—and never have I been in court where the prosecutor tells the judge who can be accepted as counsel for an accused. I'll take this case to every appellant court in our judicial system and Mr. Marino will learn that in . . ." Judge Feather held her hand out signaling Colosimo to stop.

"Yes, I understand, Mr. Colosimo. You've tried many cases in many cities. But you have never served as counsel in any of my trials. So, let me assure you, Sir, that the decision I am about to make in this case is entirely mine. Now, counsel, please take your seats."

CHAPTER SIX
Friday, February 13

Judge Feather picked up the written waivers that had been signed by Reid and McDowell and held them in her hand as she spoke. She was not completely comfortable with the decision she was about to make, but she did not want to try this case with three separate counsel only to have it reversed by the appellate court ruling that she denied the two defendants the right to their own selected counsel.

"I have advised both of you that you are waiving very important rights by making this unusual request. The importance of an independent, conflict-free, counsel in a criminal case cannot be overemphasized. It is a right guaranteed by both the U.S. and the Georgia constitutions. But you have made your choices, and I have determined that you have a right to make these choices, even against my advice. So, I am approving your requests to have Mr. Colosimo serve as your counsel. You may find it in your best interest at some later time to obtain other counsel, but unless and until you inform me otherwise, Mr. Colosimo will serve as your defense counsel."

She paused and looked at her trial calendar. "I'll hear any motions you may have on February 27 and also set the trial date." Then she looked directly at Colosimo. "Mr. Colosimo, do you have any questions?"

"No questions, but I will be submitting a demand for a speedy trial. And I mean a *speedy*. And not next term."

"I'll expect you to submit your request in writing, Mr. Colosimo, and I'll set the trial date at the hearing I'm scheduling for February 27. Is that date satisfactory with your schedule, Mr. Marino?"

"Yes, Your Honor."

"Good. Then I'll see you all in court at 9:00 a.m., February 27." And with that, Judge Feather called the next case on her arraignment calendar.

Scott picked up his laptop and some papers from the table and walked toward the exit. As he did so, he noticed someone rise from a seat in the spectator section and also begin walking toward the exit. It was Bill Baldwin. Scott was not surprised; Baldwin would have lots of questions about today's arraignment. But it was already midmorning, and Scott had a stack of cases on his desk needing attention. He walked faster, hoping it would discourage Baldwin from following him. He could field his questions on the phone and frequently did. He wasn't trying to avoid Baldwin entirely; they were professional friends, and Baldwin was often a source of needed information. He covered Chatham County criminal trials for the *South Georgia Times* and had attended all three of Scott's cases involving John Harrison, as well as the trial of Harrison's attorney, Max Gordon. Scott had answered many of Baldwin's questions about those cases, and Baldwin had always honored Scott's requests for anonymity when writing the news articles of the cases. Their relationship had proved to be mutually beneficial. It was a tip from Baldwin which had led to the arrest and ultimate conviction of John Harrison for the murder of a young woman during a robbery at a Savannah restaurant.

Baldwin caught up with Scott as he entered the hall corridor. "Scott, I know you are in a hurry to get back to your office, and I'll not try to stop you. I'm assuming you'll be meeting Jennifer at the Library after work. So, my friend, I'll just meet you two there, buy you a mug of Juri's watered-down beer, and we can talk for a few minutes. OK with that?"

"Sure, Bill, if you promise no phone calls today."

"It's a promise. I'll see you about 5:30."

Scott took the elevator up to his office. As he opened the door, he immediately saw the stacks of files and the blinking office phone. It would be a long afternoon, but he was looking forward to meeting Jennifer at the Library. Bill Baldwin would be only a short distraction.

CHAPTER SEVEN
Friday, February 13

B ill Baldwin was already at the Library when Scott arrived. He was seated at the bar, and he and Juri were in a lively discussion about the upcoming baseball season and the chances of the Atlanta Braves making the playoffs. Juri, as usual, was doubting the possibilities. He looked at the big oak entry doors and was pleased to see Scott entering and walking toward the bar.

"Braves going to struggle again this year, right Scott? Just like last year. Haven't seen any improvement in three years. Bill says they have some good new hires. You hear anything about that? Only new hire I heard about is that relief pitcher, Boone Logan, from the White Sox. But he had a 5.95 ERA; I don't think that's going to make an improvement." Juri grabbed a frozen mug from the freezer, filled it with Scott's favorite beer, and slid it down the bar. Perfect landing—directly in front of Scott as he took a seat at the bar next to Bill.

Juri was a big Braves fan and especially enjoyed discussing the Braves with Scott. Scott had attended the University of Alabama on a baseball scholarship and was selected All-SEC as a third baseman. After graduation, he was drafted by the Atlanta Braves franchise and served a couple of years in the minors. He was assigned to the Macon Braves in the Class A South League. But that was as far as he got. He had an excellent arm but batting proved to be his weak spot, and he never made it to the majors. Nevertheless, Juri always introduced him as that former Braves player and maintained a large color photo behind the bar of Scott in a Braves uniform. Juri was very proud to claim Scott as a friend.

"Thanks, perfect shot," Scott said as the beer arrived. He picked up the mug and looked at it admiringly before clinking it against Bill's half-full mug. "I haven't seen much about the new hires, Juri, but can't say I've been looking hard, either. What have you heard, Bill?"

"Not much. I know that last month they signed a Japanese pitcher who's supposed to be outstanding. But he hasn't been tested in the majors. There are a number of excellent free agents they're pursuing, but no signings yet. I know they are really disappointed with their showing in the last three years, so I expect some big money to be thrown out there soon. We'll just have to wait and see. Now I have a question for you, Scott. Just what was going on in that courtroom this morning?"

"What was going on? You were there and will probably write about it for tomorrow's paper."

"You know what I mean. Why were you fighting so hard to keep Colosimo from representing those two guys who work for him?"

"You want my public answer or the real answer? And we are off the record, right?"

"You know the drill, Scott. We are always 'off the record' unless you tell me we can be on the record. But let me hear both answers."

"The public answer is we always seek justice. Trite you may say, but it's true. We want the real bad guys in jail, and the real bad guy, in this case, is Colosimo. The other two defendants just follow his instructions. That doesn't make them innocent, just less responsible. How much of the facts surrounding this case are you aware of?"

"Just what I heard in court this morning. All three are charged with influencing witnesses and conspiracy to influence witnesses. They waived the reading of the indictments, so I don't have dates or facts. Clue me in."

"You were at the Max Gordon trial. Perhaps you recall my opening statement where I promised the jury I would be calling two witnesses who had been paid $250,000 each by Gordon to lie. We had both of them cold, with photos of them accepting the cash. Gave them good pretrials to testify against Gordon. And then neither showed for trial. One cut his leg monitor and skipped town and hasn't been seen since. We were never able to locate his cash payment, so he's now probably in some Caribbean island counting his cash. The other guy was Vijay Patel. You remember him, don't you? He was a witness at the first Harrison trial and was to be a witness at the Gordon trial."

"Sure. He runs that convenience store—Fast Eddies—out on Waters Avenue. And the way I remember him was his answer to the 'why' question asked by that incompetent defense counsel—you know, that real estate professor who was appointed counsel when the first counsel got canned by the judge early in the trial."

"Yep. The answer to that question turned my *losing* case into a winner. But in the Gordon trial, his absence turned my *winning* case into a loser. And the reason he failed to appear was caused by Colosimo and his two assistants. Reid and McDowell did just as Colosimo directed. They drove down from Atlanta, visited Patel at his convenience store, and fed him lies to persuade him not to testify. Sure, they are as guilty as Colosimo, but Colosimo is the ugly force behind all of it, and he's the one I want most."

"So, let me guess. You want to cut them a deal to get their testimony against Colosimo, right?"

"You've been hanging out in courtrooms too long, Bill."

"And you were so opposed to Colosimo serving as their counsel because it will make cutting them a deal more difficult."

"As I said, you've been hanging out in courtrooms much too long. Colosimo as their counsel will not just make it more difficult, he'll make it impossible. Any pretrial has to be submitted through a defendant's counsel. I can't deal directly with a defendant represented by counsel. I don't have any direct evidence of Colosimo's directing their trip to Atlanta, but those two would not have made a 500-mile round trip on a Monday on a whim and their own dime. Common sense should tell the jury that, but they still need the evidence."

"Next question. And this one has been puzzling me more than it should. When Gordon was going to trial, you made a motion for the judge to require—as part of his bail—that he be prevented from serving as counsel in any case until the charges against him had been resolved. You didn't make that motion in this case. No objection to 'Diamond Jim' appearing in court while under indictment awaiting trial? How come?"

"You say you recall my motion that Gordon not be allowed to participate in any trial while awaiting trial. Then I'm sure you recall Judge Vesely denied that request. I didn't like her decision, but I haven't found any authority since to support my request—and I've been looking. I didn't like the low bail that all three got in this case either, and I don't like Colosimo serving as counsel while awaiting trial. But it is what it is. He wants a speedy trial, and I'm ready to give it to him. With a conviction, I won't have to worry about his trying a case in any courthouse—ever."

Juri had been standing inside the bar, across from Bill and Scott. Suddenly he looked over at the entryway and stared. It caught Scott's attention, and he turned and looked, as did Bill. They saw Jennifer, her beautiful eyes radiating below her golden blonde hair, a broad smile on her face.

"Ah, now let's break up this serious talk," said Juri. "I've got a good story for Jennifer."

Jennifer walked quickly to the bar, gave Bill a brief hug and Scott a quick kiss. Bill moved one seat over, and Jennifer took his seat, next to Scott. Scott took her hand and held it for a long moment. He knew Juri would soon be telling one of his old, off-the-wall blonde jokes. They were usually quite harmless, and they gave Juri so much pleasure telling them he did not try to dissuade him.

"Your manners, Juri. Get Jennifer a drink," said Scott.

"Of course," replied Juri, who knew Jennifer's preference and had begun preparing it as soon as she was seen at the door. Immediately, as if by magic, he placed the drink on the bar in front of her, and stepped back a pace and stood deliberately erect—his usual stance when he began his "stories."

"This really happened," Juri said. He stepped forward and continued.

"I was at a Shell station this morning when I heard two blondes discussing the big rise in the gas prices. First blonde was filling a big Chevrolet Tahoe. She says 'I wonder how long we are going to have these high gas prices?'

"Second blonde says, 'I don't know, but I heard someone on TV say they were going to go even higher.'

"First blonde just shrugs and says, 'Won't make any difference to me; I'll just put in a few gallons at a time.'"

And as usual, Juri looks from Scott to Jennifer to Bill, waiting for a response which Jennifer gave with an eye roll, and Scott and Bill gave with thumbs down. It made no difference to Juri, who was soon laughing hard at his own joke, knowing the three would join him— the usual routine after a Juri "story." And they soon were.

Bill placed some bills on the counter, made some departing pleasantries to Jennifer and Scott, and began to walk toward the Library exit. Juri called after him.

"Bill! Wait! Want to hear about the giraffe that walked into a bar?"

Without turning, Bill just waived an open palm back toward Juri and kept walking.

Scott reached for Jennifer's hand and helped her from her seat. Several customers had taken seats at the far end of the bar. Juri walked over to take their order as Scott and Jennifer continued to the exit. They had a wonderful night planned and it wasn't at a bar.

CHAPTER EIGHT
Monday, February 16

It was 8:30 a.m., and Colosimo and Reid were in Colosimo's Atlanta office. After their court session in Savannah the past Friday, Colosimo had set a strategy session for the three of them "first thing Monday." The office opened at 8:00 a.m., but McDowell had not yet arrived.

"We can get this case behind us without too much damage," said Colosimo. "But Andy concerns me. His dawdling at the hearing Friday should concern both of us. Do you think he's on board?"

"I don't know. I believe he still thinks he can be admitted to the bar—some bar, any bar, any state. But he's flunked the Georgia Bar three times, and even if he passes, he still faces the character check. Besides being suspended from law school for one semester for some honor code violation—which you already know about—he told me he had been arrested in Alabama for some activity involving an underage female."

"I never heard about that arrest. What do you know about it?"

"He's never told me any details, but he says he was cleared of any criminal charges. I asked him what he meant by 'cleared' and he got a bit offended and told me to just drop it, so I did. His situation is different from mine. I know that with my disbarment and my arrest record in Tennessee and the Georgia conviction, I'll never be readmitted to *any* bar."

"So, you are stuck with me, doing my dirty work, right?" Colosimo was smiling and then began to laugh.

Reid smiled, but it was half-hearted. "And I guess I should be happy to have a job—any job."

"Well, Tom, you don't have just any job, you are my senior associate. And making damn good money."

"Making damn good money doing your dirty work," Reid added, with a laugh.

Colosimo's desk phone rang. It was his secretary. "Mr. McDowell is here. Shall I send him in?"

"Yes, of course. Now."

McDowell entered, apologized briefly for being late, and took his usual seat in the chair on the left front of Colosimo. Reid occupied the chair on the right. It was the same seating arrangement they had observed since McDowell joined the team some three years previous.

Colosimo looked at McDowell. "Tom and I were just discussing the strategy for getting this behind us. Since the judge approved my representation for all of us, there is no need for any change in the plan we discussed last week. Just want to make sure all are on board. For obvious reasons we are not going to record this or put it in writing."

Reid smiled and looked over at McDowell. McDowell did not return the smile. He looked attentively at Colosimo, who continued to speak.

"If we stay on course, my law firm—with both of you on board—will continue to be successful. And you two will continue to share in the profits. Our firm has been very profitable—especially over the past three years that we've been working as a team. I believe that I have been quite generous with your salaries during this time. And I now promise both of you that if our plan for defending against these Savannah charges is successful—as I'm confident it will be—I'm increasing each of your salaries by fifteen percent immediately, and at least a five percent increase each year thereafter."

Finally, there was a smile on McDowell's face, and Colosimo continued. "I want to make absolutely sure the plan and all of its implications are clear and understood by all of us. And rather than me going over the plan, let's have one of you restate it. I want to make sure we are in complete agreement. Speak up if you have any questions or concerns."

Colosimo picked up his phone and buzzed for Gay, his secretary. When she answered, he told her to hold all calls. Then he turned to Reid.

"Tom, outline the plan, as you understand it. Andy and I will respond when you are finished."

Reid turned and faced McDowell. He knew his job was to convince McDowell. He and Colosimo were clear and in full agreement.

"First, a plea of not guilty has been entered for each of us, and the plea will remain not guilty for each of us. There will be no discussion of facts and events of this case outside this office. At trial, only Andy and I will testify for the defense. Jim will not testify." Both Reid and McDowell used the name "Jim" when referring to or addressing Colosimo. Reid continued.

"My testimony will be the same as Andy's, that is, the plan to go to Savannah and discuss the case with the witness, Vijay Patel, was solely ours, because we knew our boss would not approve. This is the key ingredient of the plan—make sure there is no evidence for the jury to convict Jim. We drove down and back the same day in my car. I did not claim travel reimbursement as I would normally do because we wanted to keep Jim completely in the dark about the trip. We don't deny making the trip. How can we? They have us on the store's security camera. But there was no sound recorded. We will testify that we didn't give or promise Patel anything, and we didn't try to persuade him from attending or testifying. We only mentioned two things. One, that he would be wise to consult with another attorney who could advise him about possible defenses. And two, we told him it was very important that he tell the truth. That was all we were asking of him, to just tell the truth. We'll both deny we even mentioned possible defenses or perjury or anything other than advise him to tell the truth and get additional legal advice. That's it. Agree, Andy?"

McDowell nodded in agreement. But the nod concealed his aching discomfort with a plan that made him and Reid take the fall for a scheme planned and directed by Colosimo. He knew a conviction in this case would end any chance he now had of becoming a member of the bar in any state. Yes, he understood that it was possible they would be found not guilty. And he believed Colosimo's promise to continue his pay if sent to prison and to continue his employment—regardless of the outcome. He knew that Colosimo was the major target of this criminal action and that if Colosimo were to be found guilty, he would surely lose his license to practice law, which would mean that he and Reid both would lose their employment. The pay was good; he enjoyed his work for the firm. But during these past three years, he had visited enough of their clients in jails and prisons to get a good picture of prison life. It was frightening, and he wished he could find a way out.

Seeing Andy nod in agreement, Colosimo quickly said, "Good. Now let's get to work on that felony murder case in Conyers. We have some witnesses who need some additional details. Plus, find me one more defense witness who saw it all. Got it?"

CHAPTER NINE
Friday, February 20

Scott walked into the Library about 5:30 p.m. with a wrapped package under his arm. There were several customers seated at each end of the bar. He took a seat in the midsection. The bar at the Library was about thirty feet long, symmetrically curved and made of beautiful maple and teak wood. The top of the bar was laminated and smooth. This made it possible for Juri to perfect his skill of sliding mugs down the bar for a perfect landing directly in front of the customer. He rarely missed.

Scott had just placed his package on the bar top when he saw the cold mug heading directly toward it. He grabbed the package quickly, avoiding a collision with the frosty brew.

"Ah, that was a close one," said Juri. "What's in the package?"

"Surprise—for you. Open it."

Juri walked over and picked up the package. He began to remove the tape on the heavily wrapped package, treating it as if it were an explosive device. When he had at last removed all the paper, he grinned. It was a large framed photo of the Braves manager, Bobby Cox. And it was signed.

"To Juri, with best wishes,
Bobby Cox. February 4, 2009."

"Wow! For me?" asked Juri.

"For you. I'm been trying for months—wanted to get it to you for Christmas but was only able to make the necessary connection a couple of weeks ago."

Juri held the photo over his head, turned it slowly so all the bar patrons could see it, and loudly proclaimed, "Bobby Cox, who's going to bring the Braves to another World Series." He paused. "This year, 2009!" He then removed a beverage advertisement from the wall behind the bar and replaced it with the photo. His grin did not leave him.

"My favorite all-time major league player—played third base for the Yankees. Did you know that Scott?"

"I think I heard that somewhere. Probably from you."

"Well, he wasn't exactly a star player—had bad knees. Was with the Yankees only three years. But he is a star manager. Named manager of the year eight times by *Sporting News*. That's a record."

"He's set a number of records. One is for the number of times he's been ejected from a game by the umpire," Scott said with a laugh. "He still has the record. It's now over 150 times."

"Well, he's pretty proud of that. Most of the time he was trying to protect one of his players from being tossed. It costs him $500 each time he's ejected. Some *Sporting News* guy wrote that the last time he paid, he wrote the check for $10,000, with a note saying to let him know when that runs out. I think he knows the fans get a kick out of seeing him blow up and get tossed. He's the only player or manager to get ejected from two World Series games."

Juri walked over to serve a customer, then returned and asked, "Jennifer coming tonight?"

"Of course. It's Friday, right? Bill Baldwin will also probably be here. He left a message on my office phone, asking some questions about the 'Diamond Jim' trial. I didn't have time to return the call, so he'll probably show since he has me on his radar."

"On his radar? In his gun sight is more like it. Look behind you."

As Scott turned, he saw Bill approaching. "My favorite reporter. Sit down and you can buy us both a beer."

Bill took a seat next to Scott, and in a short moment, a cold mug of beer was sliding across the top of the bar. It came to rest two feet past where Bill was sitting.

"You missed, Juri. Beer's on you," said Bill.

"Then I'll charge you for my story," said Juri. "This is a good one."

"Then save it for a special day," said Bill. But he knew the "story" was going to be told anyway. So, he just picked up his mug, took a sip, smiled, and waited.

As usual, Juri stood up to his full height, took a step back from the bar, and looked from Bill to Scott, making sure he had their attention.

"Lady was standing at a crowded bus stop wearing a tight leather skirt. Bus stopped and it's her time to get on. Step was a bit high and her skirt a bit too tight. She couldn't lift her leg. So, she gives the bus driver a quick smile and reaches behind her to unzip her skirt a little." A smile is now covering Juri's face.

"Again, she tries to step up, but again, the skirt is too tight. She smiles again at the bus driver, reaches behind to unzip a little more.

"Once again, she tries to get on, no luck. Still too tight. So, back behind her she goes again, with another quick tug on the zipper." The smile is now a broad grin.

"Another try, still couldn't lift her leg far enough. About this time, a big Texan who was standing behind her picked her up by the waist and placed her gently on the steps of the bus.

"Lady goes ballistic, turns to the Texan and yells, 'How dare you touch my body! I don't even know you!'

"Texan smiles and in his slow drawl, responds, 'Well, ma'am, normally I would agree with you, but after you unzipped my fly three times, I kinda thought we was friends.'"

And with that, Juri's grin turned into a hearty laugh, and a look from Scott to Bill and back again, until they had joined in the laughter. It was always hard not to share in Juri's laugh, even with old worn jokes. The telling was always better than the joke.

When the laughter had subsided, Juri looked at Scott. "You did say that Jennifer was coming, right?"

"Should be here anytime."

"Good. I've got a good one for her."

Bill looked at Juri and said, "Juri, would you excuse us a minute. I've got some questions for Scott."

"Sure," said Juri as he turned and walked to the far end of the bar.

"This case isn't much on the big news radar right now, Scott. But I think it will be when it gets underway. When do you expect it to start?"

"Don't know. Don't have a trial date yet. Judge Feather will set it next Friday when we have another hearing scheduled. Colosimo said during arraignment that he was going to ask for a speedy trial."

"How soon would that be?"

"Can't say. But once he files his speedy trial request, it has to be this term of court or the next. This term ends first Monday in March, next term ends first Monday in June, so no later than May. Likely sooner. Mid-April would be my best guess—depends on the judge's calendar."

"How long do you think the trial will last?"

"I would expect no more than a week, including jury selection. I don't expect many witnesses for either side."

"Who are they?"

"Obviously, my primary witness is Vijay Patel—if he shows. He didn't show for the last trial because he was intimidated by Colosimo's thugs. He was facing some serious charges—perjury and subordination of perjury. We have photos of him smiling as he accepted $250,000 cash for his testimony. Plus, contempt for his no-show at the Max Gordon trial. But his testimony is essential, so we've given him a very favorable pretrial for a plea to one charge. We dropped the subordination charge and the contempt. He's already pleaded guilty to the single charge of perjury. Hasn't been sentenced. We asked the judge to postpone sentencing until the Colosimo trial is over. Maximum sentence for his perjury conviction is ten years confinement and $1000 fine. If he testifies truthfully at the Colosimo trial, I've agreed to ask the court for a sentence of no more than one-year confinement and a $500 fine. Like I say, very lenient pretrial."

"But isn't he taking a chance? That's not a sure thing. The judge may decide to slap him with the max."

"True, but I strongly believe the judge will agree with my recommendation. And of course, the defense believes it also. The judge in his case is Judge McCabe. He was a long-time prosecutor before going on the bench. He understands the necessity for deals like this. Besides, Patel knows I could prove the charges against him if I decided to take it to trial rather than offer him this pretrial, so he really had nothing to lose and all to gain. You've been covering trials here in Savannah for years—what do you think?"

"I think you are safe with Judge McCabe; wouldn't be sure with a couple of other judges over there."

"Our other witness is GBI agent Carl DeBickero, who made the arrests. And as far as I know, the only possible witnesses for the defense are the two hoods who got Patel to disappear, plus Colosimo himself. So, it should be a short trial unless they find some additional witnesses to purchase, as they often do. Why the early interest in this trial?"

"Readers. They are interested. Actually hungry. And it's my business to feed them. I don't have to remind you that this case grew out of the Gordon trial last November—and the shootout that followed outside the courthouse leaving two dead. That was my big story of the year."

"And you plan to milk it as long as you can," Scott replied with a chuckle.

"You bet. I'll be at the hearing next Friday for that very purpose."

"I'll see you there." Scott turned his head toward the Library entrance. "Right now I need to attend to something magic that just walked through the front door."

Bill turned to look. It was Jennifer. She was casually dressed but still radiantly beautiful. She walked quickly to Scott, gave him a kiss and whispered in his ear, "I love you. But keep it a secret." Then she turned to Bill. "Hope I'm not disturbing any plans. You two seem to be always plotting." She was smiling.

"No, I was just leaving. But nice to see you again, Jennifer."

Juri overheard the conversation. "No, you can't leave yet, Bill. I've got a good story for Jennifer. Ready?"

He was speaking loudly and all three turned to face him. They knew his "ready" was not really a question; it was a signal he was about to begin his "story." Out of habit, they turned and waited. After all, he was a good friend and he thoroughly enjoyed telling his "stories." And sometimes they were actually funny.

Juri stepped back, stood erect, and as usual, looked from side to side to make sure he had their attention.

"Blonde runs into a convenience store and tells the clerk she accidentally locked her car key in her car and asked if he had a wire coat hanger she could use to try to open the door.

"Clerk says, 'Let me look.' He finds a coat hanger and gives it to her."

Juri took a step forward and continued, a trace of a smile beginning. "After a while, the clerk looked out and saw she was still having trouble trying to open the car door. So, he goes out to help."

The smile on Juri's face got bigger. "When he got there, he heard another blonde inside the car, saying, 'left four more inches and down a bit.'" Juri's smile turned into his usual hearty laugh.

His laugh was contagious. All three joined in, at the same time giving him a unanimous thumbs down, along with the usual jeers and hisses.

When the taunting was over, Juri looked at his audience and said with a broad smile, "Ready for another one?"

"No mas, no mas," replied Scott, as he reached for Jennifer's hand and quickly departed the Library.

CHAPTER TEN

Tuesday, February 24

Colosimo was in his Atlanta law office on West Peachtree Street shortly before noon when his desk phone buzzed. It was his secretary, Gay Hess. "There is a Miss Jessica Valdez here to see you. She says it's personal and prefers not to discuss it further with me."

"Then send her in," said Colosimo.

Jessica entered, wearing a skin-tight black leather skirt, silk, raspberry-colored low-cut blouse, and matching heels. It was similar to the sexy outfit she wore to her first meeting with Scott in his assistant district attorney office a year and a half ago. And today, as then, she was a stunningly beautiful young woman.

She looked directly at Colosimo with her bright mesmerizing eyes. "I'm Jessica Valdez. I understand you are an accused as well as a defense counsel in a case in Savannah being prosecuted by Scott Marino. I believe I can help you."

Colosimo was immediately impressed by both her bold statement and her striking beauty. Though seldom lost for words, at this moment he was struggling. He slowly rose from his chair. With an open palm, he directed her to a large leather chair near his desk and tried to wrap his mind around the situation now unfolding in his office.

"Yes, please tell me what brought you here."

"Mr. Colosimo, I was once a law student a Savannah College of Law and an intern in the Chatham County DA's office. Scott Marino was my supervisor. I went to him for assistance with a research project. Instead of helping me with the project, he initiated certain actions that resulted in my expulsion from law school. I am now a real estate associate with my aunt here in Atlanta. So, I make no claim that my offer is anything other than an effort at payback to Scott Marino. It would give me pleasure to play some part in your defense. I was in my senior year when I was expelled, so I have a fair amount of legal education and have always been good at research. At least I could assist with that—and any other tasks that you may find appropriate."

Colosimo was amused, intrigued, and captivated all at once. But he was also a cautious attorney who had participated in more subterfuges, tricks, and cons than most people had even heard of. Perhaps this was merely a ruse from the prosecutor's office. While the Chatham County DA's office had a reputation of fair dealing— he had carefully checked that out so that he would not offer money foolishly—he trusted no one. New associates can change the office quickly. Yes, he was very much intrigued by this young woman and her proposition, but he would proceed slowly.

"You state that Scott Marino initiated action that got you expelled. Tell me more about that."

Jessica had hoped such additional information would not be necessary. She thought of several responses, all false, like placing the blame on a vindictive Scott after she spurned his attempt at a romantic relationship. But it would be a complicated explanation. She quickly decided to reveal the ugly truth. It would be quick and simple. The actual facts behind her dismissal from Savannah Law may be considered a plus. She had researched Colosimo's law firm. It had a reputation for underhanded and unlawful dealings, such as the defenses employed in the Gordon trial which resulted in the charges Colosimo and his two associates were now facing. So, she answered his question.

"Mr. Colosimo, I'll be truthful with you. The assistance I requested from Scott Marino was for him to sign off on a research paper. Thinking I could trust him, I admitted the work was by another law student at the University of Miami. He refused to sign off on it and advised me not to submit the paper for credit. But I was out of time to do the paper and quite desperate, so I submitted it. When he found out, he informed the law school, which conducted an investigation that resulted in my dismissal. I'm still bitter, and frankly, nothing would please me more than to see you defeat him and embarrass him at the trial you're facing. I'm willing to serve without pay and do anything necessary to see him lose this case. My father is a successful civil trial lawyer in Miami. As a result of this incident, he's essentially disowned me. It would be at least some payback for my humiliation."

Colosimo swiveled his chair to face a side wall of his office. He appeared to be in deep thought. It was a long moment before he turned again to face Jessica. She was biting her lip. Her eyes were now moist with a fiery glaze and sternly focused on Colosimo. He could see fierce determination in this young woman.

"Jessica, I may indeed find a place for you. And if I do, it will not be without pay. You will be added to the payroll. We shall see. But first I want you to meet the other two team members. They serve as paralegals and investigators—and in other capacities. You would be the only female member of the team. I want to make sure there is a fit with the team culture. I have an appointment scheduled soon, so let me see if Anderson and Tom are available to meet with you."

Colosimo buzzed for Thomas Reid, who was the senior of his two paralegal/investigators. He quickly entered the room and was introduced to Jessica.

"Tom, I am considering hiring Jessica as another team member for our firm. I don't have time now to complete the interview process. You know our needs and our . . . eh . . ." He paused, then added, "culture," and continued.

"Take her around the office. Treat her as a potentially valuable member. And she may be soon. If you have time, take her to Marlow's or the Sun Dial for lunch. Make sure you take Andy with you. Jessica, you ask all the questions you want, and Tom, you give her straight answers. We'll meet tomorrow morning, and Jessica, I'll make sure you have our answer by tomorrow afternoon. Leave your phone contact with my secretary on your way out."

CHAPTER ELEVEN
Wednesday, February 25

Thomas Reid was anxious to report to Colosimo on his interview and tour with Jessica. He met with Colosimo first thing Wednesday morning. McDowell was not present, but McDowell had been with Tom and Jessica for most of Tuesday, and as suggested by Colosimo, the three of them had lunch at Marlow's.

"I think she'll be a good fit, Jim. She's smart, and the one thing she's fixed on is helping out with our upcoming trial. Not because she loves us—hey, we just met—but because she hates the prosecutor, Marino. It's intense. I think she's willing to do whatever we need to have done. No question she'll fit in with our 'culture.'" Reid emphasized the word, then began to laugh.

"Did you explain what her duties might entail?"

"Well, she knows what we are accused of, so I think she has an idea of what Andy and I do. But no, I didn't go into any details. Besides, I'm not sure what you immediately have in mind for us. But I'm pretty sure we can depend on her for whatever needs to be done—as long as it helps to embarrasses or harass that Marino guy in some way. She wants to see him lose this case as much as we do."

"I doubt that," replied Colosimo, with a chuckle. "But it's good to hear. She told me he was her supervisor when she was a student intern at the DA's office. Did she discuss any personal characteristics or personal weaknesses of Marino? Anything that may be useful at trial?"

"She was totally negative about the guy, so I don't know that we can rely on anything. Her dislike comes through, totally. She did say he has no experience at jury selection, always relying on someone else for that."

"What does Andy think of her?"

"Impressed. He liked everything about her. Maybe too much. Couldn't take his eyes off her low-cut blouse. That concerns me a bit. Andy's young and just ended a relationship with someone he had been serious with. Former law school classmate, now a member of a civil law firm in Marietta. She dumped him right after he failed the bar for the third time. He might be a bit ripe for her picking if she finds any interest there."

"Well, we can't worry about Andy and his failed love life. Anything else you think I should know about the girl?"

"She likes red wine. None of that pinot grigio for her. We took her to Marlow's for lunch as you recommended. She's a two-glass cabernet gal."

"I like that. I'm going to call her this afternoon and offer her the job, starting tomorrow. We need to get her involved in the trial quickly. What time are we leaving tomorrow?"

"We have a Delta flight out at 4:55. Reservations at the Hyatt by the River on West Bay. Ten-minute walk to the courthouse."

"You can walk; I'll catch a cab."

Reid laughed. "Got it, Boss."

"If the new gal is able to start in the morning, you can have her start working on the brief for the change of venue motion. Need to keep her focused on this trial while we're gone. When I call this afternoon, I'll tell her to check in with you when she arrives. Make sure she sees Gay to complete the employment forms. She can start using that extra desk in Andy's office."

"I think Andy will like that." Reid rose from his chair. "Anything else?"

"Yes. Do a deep web search on that Judge Feather. See what's there that we should know about—or do about. We had good luck with what we found in the deep search on the judge in Macon. You never know what may be lurking in those dark places."

CHAPTER TWELVE
Friday, February 27

Colosimo met Reid for breakfast early Friday morning in the Savannah Hyatt restaurant. McDowell made coffee in his room and did not join them. It gave Reid an opportunity to discuss with Colosimo a matter that had been bothering him.

"Andy has been keeping pretty much to himself lately," Reid said as they waited for their order to arrive. "When he does talk, it usually gets around to the trial, with a hint that he is not sure he's making the right decision. I'm concerned he may want out of our agreement. He's said more than once that he doesn't think he could survive a conviction and jail sentence. I've assured him that there's better than an even chance we won't be convicted and a hundred percent chance you won't be convicted, assuring us of a job paying much more than anything else we could be doing. I'm not saying he doesn't trust you; he does. But in the back of his head, he thinks he could eventually pass the bar and be admitted to practice."

"Doesn't he realize that passing the bar exam is merely the first step? He still has the character and fitness test to pass, and with his record, that's quite iffy."

"He thinks he has a chance. Not immediately, but eventually. Anyway, just thought I should run that by you. Maybe we should try to make the hearing this morning as short as possible. Keep him far away from the Chatham County DAs. He may think this is an opportune time to speak to one of them. We need to get him out of the courthouse and out of Savannah ASAP. Keep him in view until our flight back to Atlanta. He's not exactly the brightest guy to graduate from law school, but he's worked for you a couple of years and knows how pretrials work. He might think this is a good time to approach some assistant DA he sees in the men's room."

"We are listed early on the hearing calendar. I'll alert the clerk that we need to get to the airport to catch a flight back to Atlanta. Exactly when does the flight leave?"

"Five twenty-five," said Reid.

"I'll tell her 'noon.' Is Andy meeting us here for a cab, or is he planning to walk to the courthouse? Last time we were here, he walked. For him, it's only about ten minutes. I don't know what it would be for me—and I'm not planning to find out."

"Last night he said the weather report was bad, and he would go with us. I told him to meet us in the lobby at 8:15."

Reid ordered a cab, and all three left for the courthouse, located less than a mile from their hotel. The morning was producing some pretty nasty weather for Savannah. It was cold, windy, and threatening rain. The courthouse, which is the home of the Chatham County Superior Court, Eastern Judicial Circuit of Georgia, was built in 1978. There were many beautiful courthouses in Georgia, with magnificent white columns, often topped with prominent cupola towers housing clocks with large hands visible for blocks. This courthouse was not one of them. The six-story concrete building was built with an emphasis on function, not style, and while not an eyesore, neither was it an attraction for the millions of visitors to Savannah each year. This had not gone unnoticed. In 2008, a nationally prominent architectural firm was awarded a contract for design of renovations for the courthouse. Until that was completed, the duty for hosting justice in Savannah courts would remain in this unimpressive but serviceable building.

Upon arrival, Reid paid the cab driver, and he and McDowell walked rapidly toward the courthouse and entered. Though the foul weather seemed to be demanding that Colosimo do the same, he lingered for a few minutes outside, near the "Flame of Freedom"— the Veterans Memorial, near the entrance. On the grassy area just behind the monument was the site of the most vivid memory of his visit in November. He had just won an acquittal for Max Gordon, one of the nation's most prestigious trial attorneys. Reveling in the victory, Gordon had invited the news media, complete with TV cameras, to a victory celebration just outside the courthouse, where he would thank "the good people of Savannah" for seeing that "justice was done" in his case. Unfortunately for Gordon, the chief witness against him, Clarence Wilborn—a co-conspirator who had previously pled guilty—was sure that justice had not been done, and there on that grassy lawn behind the "Flame of Freedom," Wilborn produced a pistol and exercised "justice" as he saw it. The bloody shootout shown live on TV involving Wilborn and the Metro SWAT team left both Wilborn and Gordon dead. Some who had observed the trial were confident that "justice" was indeed done.

The victory speech by Gordon as well as the subsequent shootout had been viewed by Colosimo from where he was now standing, just a few feet from the courthouse entrance. The entire series of events had played in his mind daily, as they were now. He had worked especially hard on that case, involving such a renowned defendant. Maybe too hard. Did he really need to send his two investigators to Savannah to convince Vijay Patel to skip the trial? How much damage could Patel's testimony really have done? He was already awaiting trial for taking a $250,000 bribe for his false testimony in the Harrison trial. No jury would believe him now. It was a trip that should not have been made. Colosimo could see that clearly now. He sighed deeply, turned, and entered the courthouse.

He went through security quickly and joined McDowell and Reid in Judge Feather's courtroom. He would, as Reid had recommended, try to make the hearing brief. He had already filed his written speedy trial motion, and today, he had only the change of venue motion to make. Unless the prosecutor had something to present, the hearing would only take a few minutes. He would heed Reid's advice and get McDowell out of the courthouse as quickly as possible.

He was in luck. Scott had nothing to present. Judge Feather pulled Colosimo's speedy trial motion from the file and held it before her.

"Mr. Colosimo, I have read your demand for a speedy trial. I have the week of April 20 available." Judge Feather looked at Scott. "Is that week clear for the prosecution?"

Marino kept a copy of his calendar on his cell phone. But he did not have his cell phone with him. He never carried his cell phone to any courtroom. Attorneys were not prohibited from carrying cell phones into court; only the use was prohibited. And should an incoming call make a cell phone ring, the consequence was severe—confiscation, fine, and a possible contempt citation. Appropriate warning signs were posted at the entrance of each courtroom. Scott saw the result of the ring from an incoming cell phone call when he was a student intern. He would never forget the scene—it was embarrassing and ugly. It was too easy to forget to turn off a phone or just make a mistake in trying. It was a lesson that stuck with him. It was simple to just have a small paper calendar for his briefcase. He opened his briefcase and quickly found it.

"That date is not exactly clear, Your Honor. But I believe I can clear it if I could have a short recess. Should take only a few minutes."

"Good. We'll take a ten-minute recess. I also have a matter that needs immediate attention."

Not exactly what Colosimo and Reid were hoping for. But they would keep an eye on McDowell. If he needed a trip to the men's room, Reid would suddenly have the same urge. The three remained seated at the defense table. Colosimo kept them occupied with plans for dinner at the restaurant he owned in North Atlanta—"Colosimo's." The dinner would be to welcome Jessica to the firm. At the news, McDowell smiled. He suggested that it be Saturday—the following day. When both Colosimo and Reid agreed, McDowell offered to extend the invitation to Jessica by phone that morning as soon as they left the courthouse. His offer was quickly accepted—planning and placing the call would lessen the chance of his having any conversation with any of the prosecutors who may be roaming the halls.

After the ten-minute recess, Scott announced that the date—April 20—was now clear. Judge Feather inquired if there was anything further from counsel.

"We have nothing further, Your Honor," responded Scott.

"I wish to make a motion for a change of venue," replied Colosimo, "and request permission to file a brief later."

"On what grounds do you make this request, Mr. Colosimo?"

"I was defense counsel in a case in this very courthouse last November. There was an acquittal, and immediately afterward, right outside the courthouse, there was a shooting. Two men, the defendant and a witness, both attorneys, were killed. I expect my name is known by most of the citizens of this jurisdiction—and they may believe I had something to do with this tragedy."

"You may submit a brief if you wish, Mr. Colosimo, but you won't get a ruling until we see how the jury selection goes. It may turn out to be no problem at all. Anything else from counsel?"

There was nothing else from either counsel. The three defendants quickly left the courthouse and caught a cab back to their hotel. The nasty weather kept them there until time to leave for their plane back to Atlanta.

CHAPTER THIRTEEN
Friday, February 27

After the short hearing in front of Judge Feather on Friday morning, Scott spent the rest of the day working in his office. In midafternoon, he placed a phone call to Luke Schaub, Vijay Patel's attorney. Patel was still facing the perjury charges for his false testimony in the Harrison case, which led to Harrison's acquittal. There was also the charge of conspiracy to commit perjury. Adding this to his failure to appear as a witness in the Max Gordon trial, Scott was sure he could put Patel away for many years. But he needed Patel's testimony, and he knew he would have to cut a deal to get it. He had discussed a deal with Schaub that would include a sentence of no more than twelve months, to be served locally in the Chatham County jail. This was the same deal that had been offered to Patel— and accepted—for his testimony in the Gordon trial. The only difference was that Scott had not required Patel to plead guilty before he testified in the Gordon case. This new agreement would require that Patel plead guilty no later than seven days after accepting the pretrial. He had provided in the agreement that it would be withdrawn if not accepted within ten days. The last day for acceptance was fast approaching, and Scott wanted an answer.

He got Schaub on the phone. "So, Luke, is your guy accepting the agreement or not?"

"Was about to call you, Scott. He signed it this morning."

"Judge McCabe has the case," said Scott. "I'll see when he can take the plea. Has to be next week. What days are you available?"

Schaub checked his calendar. "Best days would be Thursday or Friday, but we could probably work it in some other day if necessary. Just give me a day's notice, and Patel and I will be there."

As soon as Scott hung up, his phone rang. It was Bill Baldwin.

"I know you were wondering why I wasn't in court this morning. You were, weren't you?" asked Bill.

"Frankly didn't know you weren't there. You weren't the main attraction. And no one asked about you. But this call—you want to know what happened at the hearing. Right?"

"Well, not me, but you know, the paper; the readers want to know all about that case, and I don't have anything new for them, not even the date of the trial. So that, and anything else that's new."

"Sounds like you think I'm on your paper's payroll. But it's Friday, and you know where you can find me about 5:30. I'll give you the trial date—will cost a beer. If I'm in a good mood, may even throw in some motion results."

"I really hate being so easily bribed. But I'll see you there."

The early Friday nights at the Library were always looked forward to by both Bill and Scott. They always had a beer or two, chatted with Juri—often about the Atlanta Braves and their continuing problems—and listened to one of Juri's "stories," which he always delivered with animation and enthusiasm. This Friday was no exception. Bill was already present when Scott arrived and the conversation was already centered on the Braves, even though their first game—against the Phillies—was not until April. The conversation focused on the manager, Bobby Cox, now in his twenty-fourth season of managing the team. Bill was complaining that his time to hang it up was long overdue, and Juri was hearing none of it.

Scott took a seat next to Bill, and in the next moment, a cold mug of beer came sliding down the counter, stopping right in front of Scott.

"Perfect! Now that we have someone who knows something about the game, tell him, Scott. He thinks Cox is over the hill and should be fired. You know the game, what do you say?"

"I say your aim is perfect. Maybe you should be pitching for the Braves."

Bill broke in. "Bobby Cox hasn't taken the team beyond the first round of the playoffs in the last five years. Take him out, he's cooked. Done."

"He's been building the team. He knows players. He's the guy who brought in Chipper Jones. I think this is going to be the year. What do you think, Scott?"

"What do I think? I think you and Bill will never agree on this. In fact, I can't recall anything you two ever agreed on."

"Well, he likes my stories. Don't you, Bill? And I've got a good one. Ready?"

Both Bill and Scott knew the "ready" wasn't really a question. So, they both sat back on their bar stools to listen. But before he could launch into his "story," Juri looked at the entranceway and saw Jennifer walking in. He paused as she walked to the bar, and Jennifer noted the conversation had suddenly stopped as she approached the bar area.

She gave Scott a warm kiss on the cheek, looked from Scott to Juri and asked, "Did I interrupt something important?"

"Not unless you find Juri's stories important," replied Scott.

"Of course, I do," said Jessica, giving Juri a broad smile.

"But first," said Juri, returning the smile, "let me get the bride her drink." Juri had been referring to Jennifer as "the bride" since learning of her engagement in December. In less than a minute, her favorite drink was in front of her, and Juri was standing behind the bar directly in front of his three customers.

"Ready?" he began. All three in his audience remained silent, trying to suppress a smile.

"Man walks out to the street and catches a taxi just going by. He gets into the taxi, and the cabbie says, 'Perfect timing. You're just like Frank.'

"Passenger says, 'Who?'

"Cabbie says, 'Frank Feldman. He's a guy who did everything right all the time. Like my coming along when you needed a cab, things happened like that to Frank Feldman every single time.'

"Passenger says, 'Oh, there are a few clouds for everybody.'

"Cabbie says, 'Not Frank Feldman. He was a terrific athlete. He could golf like a pro. He sang like an opera baritone, and you should have heard him play the piano.'

"Passenger says, 'Sounds like he was something really special.'

"Cabbie laughs and says, 'Oh, there's more. He could fix anything. Not like me; I can't fix a squeaking door. Remembered everybody's birthday. He knew all about wine and what food went with what.'

"Passenger says, 'Wow, some guy!'

"Cabbie says, 'Great driver, too, always knew how to avoid traffic jams. Not like me, I always seem to get stuck in 'em. But Frank, he never made a mistake. His clothing was always in style, shoes always shined. No one could ever measure up to Frank Feldman.'

"Passenger says, 'An amazing fellow. How did you meet him?'"

There was now a big grin on Juri's face, and he took a step forward. "Cabbie says, 'Well, I never actually met Frank. He died . . . I married his widow.'"

And with that, Juri burst into a loud and hearty laugh, the one that always followed one of his stories. He looked from Scott to Bill to Jennifer for approval, only to get the usual boos and hisses from all. Actually, they thought this was one of his better "stories" and eventually they joined in his laughter.

When the laughter ended, Bill turned to Jennifer and said, "Will you excuse my borrowing Scott for a few minutes of business conversation? We can do it right here. It's nothing private, just need a few facts about an upcoming trial."

"The Colosimo trial?" asked Jennifer.

"Yes, that one. They had a hearing today, set the trial date, and made some motions. I was busy interviewing President Obama or maybe I just overslept. Somehow, I missed it."

"Well, if it's important I'll hear it soon enough from Scott. Just so he didn't schedule it the week following our wedding next month. I plan to be on our honeymoon at St. Simon's Island. Would be nice to have Scott with me."

"Got that covered," said Scott.

"Good. While you guys talk, I need to confer for a few minutes with Juri about the music for the wedding reception. So, excuse me." She got up and went to the far end of the bar where Juri was standing.

As soon as she left, Bill turned to Scott and said, "So what happened over in Judge Feather's court this morning?"

"Not much. Colosimo filed a Demand for Speedy Trial, and she set the trial date for the week of April 20."

"That's two months away. Doesn't sound too speedy to me."

"Like I told you last Friday, once she received the Speedy Trial motion, she has to set it sometime within two terms of court. This term ends first Monday in March, next term ends first Monday in June. She could have set it as late as May. So, pretty speedy."

"Any other motions?"

"Only one. Colosimo wants a change of venue but didn't submit anything in writing. I'm not concerned about that one. In any case, it wouldn't be decided until we tested the jury on voir dire. Colosimo apparently thinks he's notoriously famous. I doubt that a dozen people in the county know who he is—and none care. Me included."

"Anything else going on in that trial that you can tell me?"

"Nope."

"Then I'll be on my way. Thanks. You and Jennifer enjoy the evening."

Scott turned to face the entrance to the Library as Bill was leaving. He noted that Bill stopped to greet someone coming through the doorway. It was Jaak Tarras, owner of the Library Bar and Grill, and Juri's brother.

Jaak was sixty years old, six feet, two inches tall, with broad shoulders, a full head of silver-white hair and a matching, neatly trimmed mustache. He was dressed in dark gray wool trousers, cordovan loafers, and a navy wool blazer. He wore a light blue shirt under his blazer, with a colorful necktie. This was his signature style and the one his customers usually saw daily at the Library.

Jaak walked over to where Scott was seated. They exchanged greetings, and the conversation immediately focused on Scott and Jennifer's upcoming wedding. Jaak had known Jennifer longer than Scott. They met when Jennifer was an undergrad and had a project involving historical Georgia courthouses. Jaak drove Jennifer and some other students to see the beautiful old Effingham County Courthouse in Springfield, Jaak's hometown, about twenty-seven miles north of Savannah. They became and remained friends. Scott and Jennifer visited with Jaak at the Library often and considered him a close friend. So, when the wedding invitations were being prepared, Jaak was at the top of the list. They had also engaged the Library to operate the bar for the reception at the Winery following the wedding.

"Jennifer's keeping tabs on the budget for the wedding. When you get a good estimate of the cost of the bar expenses for the dinner and party afterward, please give Jennifer a call. Or call me and I'll get the numbers to Jennifer. We'll have to give the caterer a final number and pay in advance. We'll pay your *estimate* for the bar service in advance, but if it runs a bit over, we hope you could keep the service going. We'll pay the overage later when you have a final tally."

"Nope; can't do that," replied Jaak.

Scott looked surprised, shocked. But he did not respond. After a long moment, Jaak reached over and placed his hand on Scott's shoulder.

"Scott, we can't do that because the bar services and all the wine and alcohol is Juri's and my wedding gift. There will be no charge for the service at the dinner or the reception, and that includes any 'overage,' as you put it. We want you to enjoy the wedding and the reception worry-free of extra expenses. This is our way of wishing you and Jennifer a long and wonderful life together."

Scott's face went from shock to a broad smile. "I . . . I . . . don't know how to thank you, Jaak. I'm really speechless."

"And that's not a good condition for a trial lawyer. So, just let me say again, it is our pleasure, Scott. Glad we are in a position to do it."

"Jennifer's over there discussing music with Juri," said Scott, pointing. "We are going to dinner when they are finished. I'll order a couple of glasses of wine and surprise her with this news. Then we'll toast you and Juri. What great friends. Thanks, Jaak."

CHAPTER FOURTEEN
Saturday, February 28

When Anderson McDowell called Jessica on Friday to inform her of the Saturday night celebration at Colosimo's Restaurant, he also offered to pick her up and take her to the event. She accepted, and they were now on the way to the restaurant in his bright red two-year-old Chevrolet Impala sedan. She was surprised that it had a tan-colored bench seat for the driver and front passenger. Most of the newer cars she had seen had bucket seats for both the driver and the front passenger.

McDowell had seen the vehicle Jessica drove to the office on Thursday—her Mercedes SL 550 and asked about it.

"My dad bought it for me when I graduated from college."

"Nice gift. Your dad has good taste. What college?"

"Miami."

"What type of business is your dad in?"

"He's a civil trial lawyer in Miami."

"So, I guess he got you interested in law school. The Boss—'Jim,' we call him if you wonder how to address him—says you have some law school already. Planning on continuing?"

"Yes, but I'm not sure when."

"Well, if you do, don't make my mistake. Make sure you take all the courses dealing with bar exam subjects. And good, tough professors. I didn't. After the required courses, I looked for easy professors and easy subjects. Bad decision. Still having trouble with that bar exam. But sooner or later I'll make it. I just hope sooner."

"What state have you tried?"

"So far only Georgia. Three times. I studied long and hard for that last try. I thought I knew the stuff, but I've never been good at taking exams, especially multichoice exams."

"Three times? How many times can you take it?"

"Georgia doesn't limit the number and gives it twice a year. I've applied for the one this July. I'm going to take 'em till I pass. Used an Internet review course to study for the past tests. Thought I was saving money, but it didn't work out. For this next one, I'm taking a review course right here in Atlanta. It meets on Saturday mornings and twice a week at night. I think I'll do okay this time."

The parking lot was full when they arrived at Colosimo's. After circling a couple of times, they found a spot and made their way to the reception area where Reid was waiting, drink in hand. He said Colosimo was meeting with the manager about some business matters and would meet them later. McDowell and Jessica ordered drinks, and the three were seated enjoying small talk when Colosimo appeared.

"Well, I see we are all here. Andy, you're familiar with my restaurant. Why don't you take Jessica on a tour? Our table is in the Capone Room—behind a screen in a far corner. You can't miss us—take your time; no hurry. We'll order a bottle of Caymus Cabernet and save a glass for both of you."

McDowell and Jessica departed for their tour. McDowell was more than "familiar" with the restaurant; he had visited often and absorbed all the history surrounding it. They walked out to one of the large hallways, decorated in the style of Chicago's "Roaring Twenties"—marble-topped tables, Italian tapestries, copper wall sconces, and framed photos or paintings every few feet on the walls. The photos were of Chicago in the 1920s—gangsters, flappers, speakeasies, brothels, and warehouses full of barrels of bootleg whiskey—all the unintended consequences of the Volstead Act outlawing the sale and distribution of alcohol. As they walked the hallway, McDowell explained the history surrounding some of the photos. Eventually, they circled back to the large vestibule near the entrance, where there was a large photo of the original "Diamond Jim" Colosimo, approximately five feet high and three feet wide. They paused, and Jessica began to read the bio of "Diamond Jim" printed on a large brass engraving underneath the photo.

". . . *died in a hail of gunfire from a Chicago mob,*" she read out loud. "Wow. So there really was a 'Diamond Jim' Colosimo in Chicago in the 20s. I thought he used that name—and all the diamonds he wears—just for show and promotion."

"It *is* for 'show and promotion,' but there really was a Chicago 'Diamond Jim' Colosimo, who was indeed a Capone-era mafioso. I looked it up. I have no idea if he's a direct descendant as he claims, but I really don't care. He's the boss, and if he says it, I accept it for what it's worth—and in this case, not much. Get along, go along. I wasn't around him when he built Colosimo Restaurant, but I saw an old newspaper clipping about the grand opening. In it, he was bragging about the authenticity of everything—plus that he is a direct descendant of the namesake. The restaurant opened over ten years ago, and 'Diamond Jim' has honed that image since. It does make him unique."

They left the vestibule and entered another long hallway, slowly making their way to the Capone Room, but stopping occasionally to view the old photos along the walls. When they arrived at their table behind the screen, Colosimo and Reid were seated with two half-empty wine glasses. Two empty glasses were there for Jessica and McDowell, and Colosimo did the pouring.

"As promised," said Colosimo, "a bottle of Caymus Estate Cabernet. Enjoy." He held his glass out in front and the other three quickly clicked theirs against it in a wordless toast. With smiles on all faces, the celebration had begun.

The evening passed quickly with a lively and informal conversation. The business of the law firm was not discussed. Colosimo told a few jokes and received the obligatory laughs from his associates. Jessica noted that the waiter never brought the bill; after all, the owner was sitting at the table. She was pleased that she had invited herself into this law firm and been accepted. Colosimo told her earlier in the evening that she should stop by his office when she arrived for work Monday morning for details concerning her work assignment. She was looking forward to whatever that may be. But she knew she would also be busy on her telephone project. The deadline for that—March 21—was fast approaching.

CHAPTER FIFTEEN
Monday, March 2

Jessica arrived early Monday morning. As soon as she saw that Colosimo was in his office, she checked with his secretary, Gay.

"Saturday, Mr. Colosimo told me he wanted to see me this morning. Would now be a good time?"

Gay checked, and Jessica was invited into his office.

"Good morning, Jessica. Thought we should discuss further your work in our firm. As I recall, the only task assigned to you so far has been on the change of venue brief. Any progress there?"

"I have a rough draft on my computer. I'll print it out this morning and send it to you."

"Fine. We really can't expect much from that motion until we actually begin jury selection and see what the members of the panel know of my last trial in Savannah. But now, I'd like to know what you think of our firm and the team after spending time with them Saturday night at my restaurant. As I recall, Andy escorted you to and from. How did you two get along?"

"We got along okay. He's a good driver."

Colosimo found the response strange, especially so since it was said with such a flat emphasis. He wanted to know more.

"Did he discuss our defense of the indictment we are facing in Savannah?"

"He did, and I think there are some things you should know.

As he explained it, he and Tom are accepting the entire responsibility for the visit to Patel at his small store that Monday night. They hope to be acquitted but recognize there is a fairly good chance they may, in fact, be found guilty. But in any case, their testimony will absolve you of any responsibility. And should they be convicted and found guilty, their jobs with you at a very good salary are safe. That, briefly, is what he told me. Is that essentially the defense in the case?"

Colosimo paused. *This young lady surely cuts to the chase*, he thought. "Yes, that's pretty much it. And you said there were a few things that I should know. I'm listening."

"He's very conflicted. Not sure this defense is in his best interest."

I don't like what I'm hearing, but I like very much how I'm hearing it. This young lady may prove to be very valuable. "Did he discuss any alternative he may be considering?"

"No. He seemed quite confused."

"Did you try to help him understand—to 'unconfuse' him?"

"No. I don't work for Andy. I work for you. I saw no need to assist him."

Colosimo decided to also cut to the chase. "Well, a beautiful young lady and a handsome young man, two unattached professionals, riding home together after a nice party and some fine wine, late on a Saturday night, just might find some mutual attraction. Even a 'need' as you put it, to assist his 'needs.' It's been known to happen."

Jessica laughed. "Who is the 'handsome young man' you are referring to?"

"Andy, of course."

"Perhaps to some, but I did not find him handsome—or sexually appealing if that's what you were referring to."

"No?"

"No. And he came on aggressive. He walked me to the front door of my aunt's house, where I live. I expected that. But when I opened the door with my key and turned to thank him and say goodnight, he walked right in. I could see he had more on his mind than that criminal trial in Savannah. I told him he would have to leave, as I was going to bed. He put an arm around me and tried to kiss me. I pushed back and told him to please leave. He looked quite disappointed, as well as a bit shocked. But he left quickly."

"So he was attracted to you, but not you to him. Do I have that right?"

"You sure do."

"Could that perhaps change as you get to know him better?"

"I have no idea why you would ask that question, but the short answer is 'no.' The longer answer is that I find him rather shallow. His bar results—rather lack of results—are not likely to change. Neither is his physical appearance. He's a rather boring conversationist—most of it is about him and his accomplishments, which frankly I found rather limited. There just wasn't much there that interested me. Not a guy I want to spend any time with—in or out of bed." She laughed.

Colosimo clapped his hands together and smiled broadly. "Perfect!"

Jessica looked at Colosimo inquisitively but did not respond.

"You tell me you want to help any way you can. Let me tell you how you can. It may not be something you would expect or choose, but you would be using your talent to accomplish what you say you want most, that is, a complete defeat in court of one Scott Marino. Right?"

"Right. And I'm very interested."

"Could you involve yourself in romantic deception?"

"Romantic deception? Never heard the term, but I think I know what you mean. Tell me more."

"It's simple. I would like you to lead Andy along with what—well, let's call it 'expectations.' You could help by convincing Andy to stay with the plan. He obviously finds you sexually attractive. Perhaps you could feed that attraction incrementally. When I was a young man, we called it 'rounding the bases.' The goal was a home run on the first night, but we knew it could take a few weeks. I know you don't find him attractive, but he finds you attractive and that's the key. Get his hopes up—lead him to expect he will get to home plate if he sticks with the defense plan. I need both him and Tom to testify that they and they alone conceived and orchestrated the trip to convince Patel to not appear at trial. In the next few days, he could land on first base, and in a week or so, steal second. As we approach the trial, he's heading to third—and he anticipates crossing home plate after he testifies in Savannah."

Jessica found this baseball analogy rather bizarre. But she understood. She looked him squarely in the eye. "You want me to lead him on with a promise of a rollicking night in bed as the reward? Is that my work schedule?"

Colosimo hesitated before responding. "If I've offended you, I apologize. That is not a work requirement for you. Please forget I brought it up."

She was not offended. And she was sure she had the experience to take on the challenge. In fact, it sounded like fun. She could play this game, but she sure as hell would not end up in bed with that jerk.

She smiled at Colosimo. "No problem. I can handle the task."

CHAPTER SIXTEEN
Thursday, March 5

Tom Reid and Anderson McDowell were out of the office, hunting down—and perhaps buying—witnesses for two related trials scheduled in Macon, one to begin March 9, and the second to begin the following week, March 16. Jessica was working alone in the office she shared with McDowell. "Working" was somewhat of an overstatement. The only office work that had been assigned to her was the change of venue motion—which had been completed—and research dealing with character evidence. Evidence of prior bad acts or crimes was generally inadmissible, although it might be admissible in special circumstances. Both McDowell and Reid had prior convictions, but neither had revealed specifics to Jessica and she had not asked. Usually, the issue came up in drug and sex crimes but could arise in the prosecution of other crimes. She had completed her research on the issue Monday, quickly completed a memo on what she had found, and used the last couple of days for personal research as she saw fit.

It was an opportune time. And she had the room and computer all to herself. She was skilled in social media, including Facebook, LinkedIn, Myspace, and Tumblr. She found some of the telephone numbers and email addresses she needed from those sites. And for those she could not locate, she used Internet phone directory services. Some services were free. The free services generally provided landline-only numbers, and those would not be useful for her plan. To get cell phone numbers required that she engage services that charged fees, payable in advance by credit card. She was more than willing to pay. She used all such services she could find, and by noon Tuesday, she had most of the phone numbers and email addresses she needed.

Tuesday afternoon and Wednesday, she continued to work social media sites to find phone numbers she was still missing, and for those she still could not find, she made a few personal phone calls. By Thursday afternoon her list was almost complete. She was seated at her desk, scrolling through her aunt's business website, when McDowell entered the room.

"Hi, Jessica. Tom and I just got back. Missed us?" He smiled, then laughed.

As soon as she saw him, she was reminded of her primary task as assigned by Colosimo. She returned the smile and replied, "As a matter of fact, I did. Missed you especially."

McDowell was walking toward his desk but stopped quickly. He turned and faced Jessica with a broad smile and a surprised look. "You did?"

"I did."

"Then let me make it up to you. Join me for a drink after work, and I'll tell you about our trip to Macon. Are you familiar with the Eleventh Street Pub?"

"No, never been there. You can drive."

"My pleasure."

CHAPTER SEVENTEEN

Friday, March 6

S oon after leaving work on Friday, Scott picked up Jennifer in his old but well-maintained 1984 Chevy Camaro, and they were on the way to visit Jennifer's mom and dad in Hilton Head. It was a trip they made frequently and one Scott especially enjoyed. He genuinely relished the company of his future inlaws, and they always made him feel welcome. He and Jennifer usually found a vibrant, sometimes romantic, restaurant to visit alone on Saturday night, and Jennifer's dad, Patrick, would always display his grilling skills on Sunday afternoon before they returned to Savannah. For this visit, Scott had already made reservations for Saturday night at the Old Fort Pub, on the water overlooking Skull Creek and the wildlife refuge on Pinckney Island.

As soon as they arrived, Jennifer's mom, Sally, asked for an update on anything related to the wedding.

"Nothing new, Mom, except I've added a couple more names to the list of those attending. That makes the total of eighty-two—and that includes everyone, including you and Dad."

"Last count you also said 'eighty-two.' But you just said you had added a couple."

"Yes, added a couple and a couple added to the 'can't make it' list."

"Well, it's OK. The caterer said a few more wouldn't make any difference. I don't have to notify them unless at least five or more are expected. I called them a few days ago to ask about servers. I was told there would be two to set up and help as long as we needed them. They have catered a number of times for events at the Winery. They said they know the layout and will be ready to start serving at 5:30. Two hours of service is built into the catering fee. That should be sufficient."

"Juri says he will have the bar set up and ready to go at 5:30 also," said Scott. "I spoke with Pastor Bacon about these times. He said that seemed about right to him. Jennifer and I have an appointment with the pastor Tuesday night to discuss the ceremony. I'll let Jennifer do all the discussing with the pastor—as long as she says 'I do,' I'll be happy."

Jennifer smiled. "Then you'll be very happy."

"Where will your mother and sister be staying while in Savannah, Scott?" asked Patrick.

"I made reservations at a bed and breakfast near Forsyth Park. My mom visited Savannah several times when my aunt—her sister— was alive, and she mentioned the park as one of her favorite places to visit. It's within a short walk."

"Would you like us to pick them up for the trip to the Winery?"

"Thanks, Patrick, for the offer, but I want to drive them there. But if you would drive them back, it would great—Jennifer and I will be leaving directly from the Winery for . . . well, it's our secret." Scott laughed.

Scott addressed Patrick by his first name but still addressed Jennifer's mom as "Mrs. Stone." Maybe later she would be "Sally," but now she was "Mrs. Stone."

Jennifer had called earlier that day asking her mom to make sandwiches for their arrival. Jennifer's mom's sandwiches were always a meal themselves, so they did not go out for dinner on Friday. But later that evening they did take the short drive to the beach, where they took off their shoes and walked barefooted along the water's edge. It was a tradition. Sometimes they would come at night, bring a blanket, and spread it comfortably on one of the soft sand dunes. They would lie there together listening to the splashing of the waves, expressing their love, and enjoying the physical wonder of each other—a world of theirs alone.

Sunday afternoon Patrick fired up the grill for his always welcome cookout ritual. He used a charcoal grill—none of this gas-fired Home Depot stuff for this grilling expert. When the coals were just right, he placed four small black sea bass on it, already prepped with his special—and original—grilling sauce. Scott never asked about the recipe. He knew he could never do it justice with his limited grilling skills, but he noted that on the table beside the grill were small containers of oregano, paprika, and garlic powder, as well as a bottle of extra virgin olive oil. He thought of asking Patrick the difference between "virgin" and "extra virgin"—sounded like comparing "pregnant" and "extra pregnant." But maybe this wasn't the best time to test Patrick's sense of humor.

Instead, he said, "Patrick, this is the last time we will be talking before the wedding. Do you have any advice for your soon-to-be son-in-law?"

"I do. And I will make it short and simple. As you know, Jennifer came along late in our marriage. We thought we could not have a child. We both sought medical advice from experts across the country. And then, to our great joy, we were blessed with Jennifer. Now we feel doubly blessed that Jennifer has brought you into our lives. And as I say, my advice is quite simple, and it is something that will bring you joy as well as sustain you in the less than perfect times all marriages bear. Just do this: at least once each day—bedtime is perfect—give her a kiss and quietly say, 'I love you.'"

Scott and Jennifer were soon on their way back to Savannah, Patrick's advice lingering in Scott's mind. *Great advice—but I already do that.*

CHAPTER EIGHTEEN
Monday, March 9

Monday morning, Jessica was in the office she shared with McDowell, trying to pull up the few telephone numbers that so far had escaped her search. She had not been assigned any specific projects and was pleased to have the time as her own. Reid and McDowell were in Augusta, Georgia, interviewing witnesses for a high-profile manslaughter case involving a prominent politician. The trial was scheduled for the week of April 6, just two weeks before their own trial in Savannah. That was also the week of the Masters Tournament at the Augusta National Golf Course. By the time Colosimo accepted the task of defending the manslaughter charge, hotel accommodations were unavailable that week in Augusta and for miles around the city—at any price. In addition to finding and interviewing character witnesses for the trial, the two were tasked with finding a nice hotel not too far from the courthouse for Colosimo and his team. The latter task was actually more formidable than the first, but money would prove helpful in both cases.

Midmorning, Jessica's phone rang. It was Gay, who informed her that Colosimo wanted to see her when she had time. *When she had time?* That struck her as rather funny, and she was still smiling when she entered Colosimo's office a few minutes later.

"Well, so glad to see you, Jessica. I've sent my guys on to Augusta for a few days. Did Tom give you anything to work on while they're gone? I told him it was his task to assign you projects for the firm, but I don't want you to be overworked."

"I'm OK; nothing I can't handle."

"Good. But that's not the only reason I wanted to see you. And have a seat. I'm going to ask Gay to bring in a pot of coffee. What do you take with your coffee?"

"I drink mine black," Jessica said, as she took a seat in a stuffed leather chair just a few feet from Colosimo.

"Same here. Never understood putting cream and sugar into a great cup of coffee. And Gay makes great coffee. I've never asked her secret, but she never fails."

"She seems to be efficient in all she does, at least that's my observation."

"Well, your observation is correct. Until December, I had two secretaries, but with Gay being so effectual, she was all I needed. So . . ." Colosimo paused.

Jessica finished his sentence. "You let the other one go."

"That's right. Two days before Christmas, I called her in and said 'Sayonara.' Sorry, it had to be at Christmas time—but I gave her a nice Christmas bonus. I have a good team, Jessica, and I'm glad to have you join us. I keep close tabs on what is going on in the way of trials, but I'm not up to date on what Tom has you doing. I haven't heard how he's working you into our system. And that's why I called you in here this morning."

Jessica did not respond. She waited for Colosimo to continue.

"We've made trying criminal cases into a science. We rarely lose, and those we do lose were lost before we got involved. And we can turn some losers into winners with our system. We represented a county commissioner last year that was a loser before we got involved—child pornography case. I hate getting involved in those. Hard to find a sympathetic juror before or during trial. But we turned that case around, and he's still serving the good folks of his county—but short a couple hundred grand from his bank account." Colosimo chuckled, then continued.

81

"We started the process early with the jury list. Andy and Tom spent a lot of time shepherding that case. By the time the jury reported for trial, we knew more about each of them than they knew about themselves. Jury was out less than an hour—not guilty. As I say, we have a system, and I want you in it."

"Well, I'm all in," said Jessica. "Tom hasn't been around much during the day to fully explain what I need to do to contribute, but I have a few projects." Jessica hoped Colosimo would not inquire about those "few projects," as she had none. But she was confident she could create a few that would satisfy him.

"Good. But I want you to know your primary assignment is what we discussed last week. How is that coming?"

"It's on track. And don't worry, I'm quite aware of my primary assignment. I'm rather intrigued by the challenge."

"Any specifics you care to share?"

"Sure. He was out of the office last week until Thursday. He asked me out for drinks after work at the Eleventh Street Pub. I told him I had never been there, so I asked him to drive. Actually, it was fun. I had a great time at the pub, despite my date—I guess you can call it that. Lots of friendly folks watching sports, laughing and having a great time. I like meeting new people, joking and having a nice glass of wine. I made sure Andy remained reasonably sober—he was driving. But when we finally left the pub—about ten or so, he drove to his apartment instead of taking me back here to pick up my car. I knew what he had in mind and quickly squelched it."

"Did that upset him?"

"No, because I've handled those situations before. I just told him I was not a one-night-stand girl. Maybe if our relationship develops, we could . . . well, he got the idea. He drove me back here and asked if he could see me Friday night."

"So, you went out again on Friday?"

"No. I told him I was busy, even though I wasn't. I didn't want this to progress too quickly in his mind. Besides, two nights in a row with Andy McDowell is more than I can handle." Jessica laughed.

"You seem to have a good handle on the matter. Can't emphasize too much the importance of your assignment. When you were out with him Thursday, did he mention anything about the trial he's facing—we're facing—in Savannah next month?"

"Yes, a couple of times. He knew I had attended Savannah College of Law, and he asked a few questions about the law school and the city. He said he had always enjoyed visiting Savannah, such a beautiful city. Then he paused for a long moment before adding, 'But I dread that next trip.' We were on our way in his car to the bar. He took his hands off the steering wheel for a moment, then slammed them both down hard a couple of times. 'Sorry,' he said, 'I'm just frustrated.' He said he really wondered if accepting the full blame for the witness tampering charges was smart on his and Tom's part. I reached over, put my hand on his shoulder and just said it made a lot of sense to me. And that we could discuss it some time, but let's just go to the pub and have a good time. He nodded his head in agreement and didn't bring it up again for the rest of the evening."

"Have you seen him since?"

"Yes. After I told him I was busy Friday night, he asked me out for Saturday. I told him I was taking my aunt out to a movie that she had been wanting to see, but if he wanted to join us, he could. I was sure he would turn down the offer, but he accepted. And he offered to drive. I'm presently living with my aunt on Lenox Road, so he picked us both up and took us to the movie at Phipps Plaza. Had a nice evening—well, considering the circumstances. My aunt thought he was a nice guy. And of course, he is—for a movie date. But . . ." Jessica laughed.

"Looks like you have things under control. I can't overemphasize the importance of your assignment. I have some calls I must make now, but I would like you to stop by after lunch, say about 2:00. I think it's important that you know a bit more about your assignment."

"Sure. I'll be here—at 2:00."

CHAPTER NINETEEN
Monday, March 9

Jessica knocked promptly at 2:00 and was invited in. Colosimo pointed in the direction of the big leather chair a few feet from his desk. Jessica sat with her arms resting lazily on the chair's arms. She deliberately tried to look casual and unconcerned, but in fact, she was quite anxious. She recalled from the morning visit that he said it was important and concerned her "assignment." The only assignment he had given her was to continue to keep Andy interested in her—with unfulfilled but great expectations. That she could do.

"I just want to underscore the importance of what I've asked you to do, Jessica. And I think I can best do that by informing you of the substantial rewards for its completion. Tom tells me he believes you are planning to continue your law school education. Are those your plans?"

Jessica was relieved. Her "assignment" was not the subject of this visit—just some reward for its completion. "Yes, but it may be a bit difficult getting back into law school. You are aware that I was dismissed from Savannah Law for plagiarism. While my grades up to that point were quite good, I'm very concerned about any law school giving me another chance."

"Well, I can fix that. Not only can I assure you admission to law school, but I'll pay for it and reserve a spot here in my firm when you graduate."

Jessica looked surprised. Her arms, which had been resting so casually on the armrest of her chair, tightened, and she turned her fingers inward to make a lightly closed fist. She leaned forward toward Colosimo, wide-eyed in anticipation. But she did not respond.

"I don't make promises I can't keep, Jessica. I'm on the Board of Directors for Adam Lansky Law School here in Atlanta. Have you heard of it?"

"Yes, but I know nothing about it."

"That's because we're so new. We are now just in our third year. But we've received provisional accreditation from the ABA, and I'm confident we'll eventually receive full accreditation. We have the funding and the backing of some of the top movers and shakers in the legal community. We have an experienced dean, and we've hired some top professors from nationally prominent law schools. You see, when I say we have the funding, I mean real, substantial, funding. You've heard of the school's namesake, attorney Adam Lansky, haven't you?"

"I've heard the name, but that's all."

"He and I were classmates at Atlanta Law School many years ago, before it folded. We graduated together. Adam went into civil law. He got in early on both tobacco and asbestos litigation. Made a killing. I didn't come close to Adam in income, but in my field of criminal law, I did well. And at one point in Adam's career, he needed a good criminal lawyer, and he called on me. We had a good outcome, and we became close personal friends. Adam is one of the richest men in Georgia, and we have our share. I'm sure you know of Anne Cox Chambers, easily the richest person in Georgia, and her nephew, James Kennedy, second best. Both received their money from the Cox news media business, both muli-billionaires. Atlanta's got a lot of billionaires. Some you've probably heard of and some who keep a low profile. There's Bernard Marcus and Arthur Blank. They got rich as co-founders of Home Depot. Summerfield Johnston, Jr., made it with Coca-Cola, and the two Rollins brothers—Randall and Gary—got their billions from Orkin Pest Control.

And Brothers Dan and Bubba Cathy made theirs with Chick-fil-A. All Atlanta billionaires. Oh, forgot. Add Ted Turner to that group. You've heard of him, haven't you? I think he married some movie star. You recall who that was?"

"I believe it was Jane Fonda," responded Jessica.

"Oh yes; Jane Fonda—'Hanoi Jane'—the Viet Cong tank gunner. Remember that photo?"

Jessica looked confused and did not respond.

"Sorry. I realize that was before your time. But I was listing Georgia billionaires, and old Ted Turner makes the grade. But back to Adam Lansky. I'm not sure where he ranks, but he's easily a billionaire. As I said, I've known him since our days at Atlanta Law School. He loved Atlanta Law. Made several substantial contributions to it before it closed."

Colosimo stopped and looked carefully at Jessica. "You aren't from Atlanta, are you, Jessica? Miami, if I recall correctly."

"Yes, Miami."

"So, I'm sure you haven't even heard of Atlanta Law School or any of its graduates."

"Can't say that I have. But there's a lot about Atlanta that I've missed. Maybe you have some stories?"

"Not really stories, but I think you should know something about its graduates. Kind of explains why Adam Lansky funded his new law school—he thinks it's a model for how the law should be taught. Atlanta Law was in existence for over a hundred years before closing. First Atlanta female lawyer was a graduate, as well as Georgia's first female member of Congress. Over six thousand graduates before it closed. It was really a lawyer's law school—half the faculty were local practitioners. The school wasn't ABA-accredited, but the faculty taught us what we needed to know to be successful lawyers. We were proud of the way the school prepared us. And none prouder than Adam. We were ready to practice law the day we graduated, and until the Georgia Bar changed the rules, we could take the bar upon graduation. But sometime in the 1990s, the Bar decided that graduation from an ABA-accredited law school would be a requirement before taking the bar exam."

"And that led to the law school closing?"

"No doubt about it. We weren't accredited, and the school didn't have the funds necessary to get it accredited. The major expense was going to be all new facilities, including a big library. Hell, we didn't even have a little library. We just bought our books from the Emory Bookstore and went to classes in a rented building. Our professors—all judges or practicing attorneys—explained the law, and we absorbed it. But the new bar requirement shut down that teaching method. But that was also the event that led to the Adam Lansky Law School. You see, Jessica, Adam and his wife were married almost fifty years when she died. They had no children. Adam has a few distant heirs, none he knows well or wants to know well. So there he is, with lots of money to spend and still in good health. He had no favorite charity, but he had great admiration for Atlanta Law School and how it prepared him and so many young men and women for the practice of law. So he decided to start his own law school with his wealth to back it. He could enjoy watching it succeed while he was still alive. Give it to charity and he would have no knowledge of really what happened to his hard-earned cash."

"So, we now have Adam Lansky Law School, and you are on the board. And you think you can get me admitted?"

"I don't 'think' I can; I know I can. And I've prepared a contract with this in mind. Here, look it over, Jessica." He handed a paper to Jessica. He was smiling.

Jessica began to read the one-page document. It was in the form of a contract for services but did not spell out any specifics of her services. She read it again, very slowly. It promised her admission to Adam Lansky Law School with paid tuition, books, and a $2,000 monthly maintenance check "upon satisfactorily completing the assignment." It bore Colosimo's signature. She soon realized that this was simply a promise of what to expect if Andy testified according to the compact. That was her assignment, her only assignment—make sure Andy testified absolving Colosimo of any blame. This odd document obviously was not a contract she could enforce, but it was Colosimo's way of spelling out her reward for the successful completion of her "assignment." It was to keep her focused and assured. She nodded in agreement, returned Colosimo's smile, folded the document and placed it in her purse.

"Now that's settled, we need a way to keep in touch. I'll be in trial in other cities during much of the time before the trial in Savannah. I want you to have access to my personal cell phone. I have another phone for business. But I want you to use my personal phone. We'll communicate by text messages, personal phone to personal phone. Let me call you now on your phone. Do you have it with you?"

She did, and she removed it from her purse. She gave him her phone number, and he immediately dialed her phone. She answered and quickly hung up. Then she sent him a text message of two words to his personal phone.

"Contract accepted."

CHAPTER TWENTY
Friday, March 13

I t was a little after 5:00 on a rainy but busy Friday afternoon at the Library Bar and Grill. The Savannah Law intra-mural football championship had just finished, and the Pigdogs were celebrating their win over the Strawberry Frogs. The highlights of the game were being repeated and embellished by the Pigdogs, while the Frogs were busy slamming the referees and offering the bad calls and the bad weather as their excuse in losing their first Spring Championship game in three years. Still, the end of the fierce competition was being celebrated peacefully with pitchers of beer and platters of pizza. The Savannah Law football championship celebration held at the Library each year was one of Juri's favorite days, and he personally delivered many of the orders, congratulating the winners and consoling the losers.

Bill Baldwin sat alone at the bar nursing a beer, well removed from the festivities but observing and enjoying the raucous celebration. Sporting events were where Bill cut his teeth as a reporter, and it made no difference that this one was a rank amateur event. He would probably report on it in "Scene from the Bleachers," a weekly column for the *South Georgia Times* that he had been writing since coming to Savannah some fifteen years ago. He wrote a column with the same name for *The Red and Black* while attending the University of Georgia. His assignment at the *South Georgia Times* was not in the sports department, but the sports editor welcomed his column, at first as a filler and later as a standard feature as it became a favorite with the readers. It consisted of whimsical, odd and off-beat sporting news, sometimes local, sometimes national, but always cleverly written. And he wished he had a dollar for every letter or email he had received over the years suggesting he correct the spelling in the title of his weekly column.

As he sat observing the celebration at the far end of the Library, he took out his ever-present pen and note pad and began scribbling. In a few moments, he looked up and saw Scott coming through the big oak entry doors. Bill smiled as Scott walked toward him and took a seat at the bar next to him.

"Well, my soon-to-be-tamed friend, how are the wedding plans going? Busy?"

"Mildly. But Jennifer is up to her . . . well, she's doing most of the planning and calling. Making all the decisions. All I have to do is show up."

"Yes, and extremely important—the highlight of your life—which must mean all the rest is downhill."

They both laughed. Then Bill added, "But you are so lucky, Scott, in finding Jennifer and convincing her to put up with you for life. But I'm sure you realize that. Is she meeting you here tonight?"

"That was the plan, but she called earlier and said she just had too much to do—a combination of schoolwork and wedding plans—so I'm picking her up at her place about 7:00 for dinner."

"So, you have a few minutes to give me an update on the Colosimo trial. What's the latest?"

"Nothing new. It's still on track for April 20."

"Any new motions from the defense?"

"They have been surprisingly quiet," said Scott. "We still have the change of venue motion to deal with, but that'll have to wait until we try to select a jury. I don't think there's much there. I doubt anyone in Savannah has an opinion one way or the other about the defendants."

"And they don't seem to be taking the trial seriously."

"What do you mean by that?" asked Scott.

"They're taking on new cases throughout Georgia, especially in the Atlanta area. And Colosimo already has a case defending a prominent politician in a manslaughter case in Augusta just two weeks before your trial. A lot of witnesses. Could last ten days or so."

"Interesting but not too surprising. Where do you get your information?" asked Scott.

"Reporter friends doing the same kind of leg-work that I do—courthouse coverage. We have our own website where we trade news on any subject anyone posts. Colosimo is a longtime 'subject.' There's a guy with the *Atlanta Journal* that posts something on him every few days. He was in trial in Macon this week and has another trial in Macon next week. The trial this week ended Thursday with a not guilty verdict. Got that from a post by our guy at the *Macon Telegraph*. Any chance for the same verdict next month in Savannah?"

"*Any* chance? I would say a damn good chance. It's a weird case. I've never prosecuted a case where a defendant acted as his own attorney. Normally, that would be a plus for the prosecution, but here the defendant acting as his own attorney *is* an attorney. Not only that, he's the attorney for the two other co-defendants. I may be the first prosecutor in the country who has tried such a case. And even if I get a conviction, it's ripe for reversal on appeal on that issue alone. The only positive thing about this trial is that it should be short. I have only four witnesses, and the defense has only the three defendants."

Baldwin smiled. "You mean they'll not be calling any character witness to testify about their great community service and unblemished character?"

"Well, so far they haven't given me any witness list. They have to do that at least five days before trial. But unless they buy a couple of witnesses—and that wouldn't surprise me—they will have a difficult time finding anyone to testify favorably on their character. One of the associates has been disbarred and Colosimo has more professional enemies than friends. I'm still checking into the background of the second associate—the law school grad who can't seem to pass the bar exam."

At that moment, Scott heard a familiar sound—a mug of beer sailing his way on the bar counter. It stopped directly in front. He looked in the direction of the sound and saw Juri walking toward them with another mug in his hands. He placed it in front of Bill Baldwin.

"My apologies, Scott, Bill. I've been busy helping with the celebration. One of our barmaids called in sick and I'm in dual mode. But I have a story for you." A broad smile soon enveloped his face.

Scott and Bill just returned the smile and waited.

Juri took a step back from the bar counter. The smile continued on his face, and his eyes were in sync with the smile. It was the facial expression that was always present when Juri began one of his "stories."

"Skeleton walks into a bar," he began. "The bartender says, 'Hi, Sam, what will you have?'

"Skeleton says, 'My usual. A beer and a mop.'"

Juri looked from Bill to Scott and back again, the smile on Juri's face broadening. Bill and Scott turned to each other, expressionless. Then Juri broke into his usual hearty laughter. Smiles slowly covered the faces of both Bill and Scott, and soon they were joining in the laughter.

"Hard day at work," said Scott. "Took me a minute."

"Skeleton jokes rattle your cage?"

"That's enough Juri. In fact, too much." Scott shook his head and began to laugh again.

CHAPTER TWENTY-ONE

Saturday, March 14

McDowell picked up Jessica at her aunt's house for a promised evening of dinner and dancing. Earlier in the week, he had asked her to join him for a weekend at a cabin on Lake Lanier. To make that offer more acceptable, he told Jessica to invite her aunt to join them. A weekend out on Lake Lanier was appealing to Jessica; a weekend on Lake Lanier with Andy McDowell was not. But she knew her "assignment," and a simple rejection of the lake invitation was not an option. She told Andy she had promised to assist her aunt Saturday with her real estate business and how disappointed she was not to be able to go. But she hoped they would be able to go out Saturday night. Andy took the rejection well, smiling broadly and telling Jessica he would make it a special evening of "dinner and dancing."

He didn't tell her where they were going for the evening, but when they arrived, Jessica was pleased. It was the Loca Luna Restaurant, which specialized in tapas, cocktails and live Salsa music. Having lived in Miami for so many years—with four years as a student at the University of Miami—she was familiar with the Latin cuisine and the music. She had spent many Friday and Saturday nights dancing at night clubs and lounges in Miami and Miami Beach. She had not danced in a long time, but still recalled all the steps in the Salsa, Samba, Bachata, and Conga. She coached Andy out on the dance floor, and he was a willing student and a fast learner.

They both had a great time and it was almost midnight when they left. The restaurant was very close to Piedmont Park, and Andy drove his car directly there and began to slowly circle the large lake in the center of the park. Although there was little moonlight because the moon was just rising, the weather was fair and the illumination from downtown Atlanta was sufficient to reveal the natural beauty of the park in the spring. The conversation was about the wonderful evening at Loca Luna—the food, the music, the dancing, the friendly restaurant staff and the couples they had met. Office work had yet to be mentioned during the evening.

Suddenly Andy pulled his vehicle to the side of the road, where there was a dim view of the lake. He cut the engine and turned to face Jessica. He just looked directly at her without speaking.

It did not catch Jessica by surprise. She expected that he would make a physical move on her at sometime during the night, and she was prepared. At this stage in her "assignment," a kiss would be both expected and appropriate. After all, her assignment was to keep him interested in *her*—and not the upcoming trial—with promises of wonderful things to eventually come. She would give him a kiss to remember. She was good at that.

But Andy did not make a move. "Jessica, I would like to discuss something with you," he said. "I would like your opinion."

"Sure, Andy, what is it?"

"It's the trial. It's constantly on my mind. I continue to wonder if my part of the deal is in my best interest or only in the best interest of our boss."

"What do you consider to be 'your part of the deal'?" Jessica knew the answer but thought she should take some active role in the conversation.

"Take the witness stand and accept the blame without involving Jim."

"And Jim's part of the deal?"

"Keep me employed, increasing my salary by fifteen percent immediately, and at least a five percent increase each year thereafter."

"Wow! Pretty good deal I would say. Especially with the good chance you have of an acquittal. Have your cake and eat it too."

"But this is a felony case, Jessica. And I didn't plan that visit to Patel. The plan came from Jim. Even the time of day to approach him at his store. The message came from Jim. Tom and I were just the messengers. I'm pretty sure I could cut a deal with the prosecutor and get myself out of this mess entirely. If I'm convicted, I would never have a chance of admission to any bar."

Jessica wanted to say, *How's that working for you now, Andy?* Instead, she said, "You tend to accept the worst-case scenario. You are not there yet and not likely to be there. And if it should happen, you have a job that you are good at and paid well for. You accepted the deal. Gave your word. You don't know for sure that you could deal with the prosecutor. Besides, I like my men to keep their word. You understand that, don't you?"

Jessica began to smile. She kept her eyes gazing into Andy's. Andy's Chevy came with a front bench seat with no center console, so there was no obstacle between them. They held the gaze for a long moment, then she reached over to Andy and pulled him close to her. Her lips went to his, and she gave him the kiss he would indeed remember.

The embrace remained for a long moment before she pulled away and smiled at him again. "That was nice," she said. "You keep your deal, and we'll keep ours. I look forward to getting this trial behind us so we can spend some *quality time* alone." She winked.

Andy returned the smile and nodded his head as a sign of agreement. He started the car, and they left the park. He drove to her aunt's house, and during the drive, the trial wasn't mentioned again.

CHAPTER TWENTY-TWO

Sunday, March 15

Jessica lingered in bed Sunday morning. She was reflecting on the previous evening, considering how to word her report to Colosimo. She hoped she had nipped in the bud Andy's thoughts of possibly cutting a deal with the prosecutor. But she knew he had real concerns about taking the rap for Colosimo. He likely could indeed, as he had said the previous night, "cut a deal with the prosecutor" and get himself out of the mess entirely. She also knew that was exactly what she would do under the circumstances. It was something she was going to have to monitor closely until the trial. And it might take more than her professional-grade kiss to do it.

This would be her first report to Colosimo since they exchanged text messages the past Monday. She wanted to be factual. Andy was really conflicted, or at least was before their lake-side chat just hours ago. She didn't want to sound alarming, but her boss needed to know, and she had promised to keep him informed. She reached for her phone on the bedside table and began tapping her text message.

"Date w/Andy last night. Dinner & dancing.
On way home he stopped, parked. Had serious chat
about trial. Has concern conviction would end
all chances for bar admit. I assured him conviction
no sure thing and yr offer was 2 good 2 turn down.

Soothed him with some light lovemaking. In your terms,
he got to 1st base! Ha. Ha. I think I can keep him
running the bases until the trial!"

She reread the message. It was a bit longer than planned, but she did not want to take the time to edit. Better to get it off early today, as she knew Colosimo had a trial starting Monday morning out of town.

She did not expect a reply, at least not today. But soon after she was dressed and at the breakfast table, her phone beeped with a text message from Colosimo.

"Keep him in the infield!"

CHAPTER TWENTY-THREE

Friday, March 20

It promised to be a busy day for Scott. He was up early, packing his suitcase for the trip he and Jennifer would be taking to St. Simons Island after the wedding. He loaded it into his 1984 Z28 Camaro and drove to the auto rental agency where he would be renting a sedan for a couple of days. The rental agency had agreed to allow him to park his Camaro on their lot and pick it up after the wedding. His rental was a five-passenger Chevy Malibu. This would serve two purposes. He needed a larger vehicle to pick up his mother and sister from the airport and also drive them to the Winery for the wedding—his Camaro was only a two-seater. But just as important, he needed a place to keep his Camaro safe from the shaving cream graffiti and other pranks his young friends in his office were sure to inflict on "the getaway car"—or what they expected to be the getaway car. He had seen first-hand "getaway cars" marked up with "washable ink." The ink was indeed "washable" but not "removable." He was determined to protect his prized possession, his Z28 Camaro. He could take out insurance on the rented vehicle to cover such damage.

Scott had been up late Thursday night waiting for his best man, Dan Koleos, to arrive. Dan had driven over 700 miles from Allentown, Pennsylvania, arriving in the early hours of Friday and was asleep when Scott left earlier that morning. Dan was Scott's roommate and fraternity brother for three years at the University of Alabama and like Scott, a star player on the university's baseball team. He was about the same height as Scott, with broad shoulders, and an all-round muscular build. He wore his red hair neatly trimmed with a stylish, close-cut beard. He and Scott graduated the same year, and both were drafted by major league baseball teams. Scott was picked by the Atlanta Braves for his quick and reliable glove work and strong arm, Dan by the Philadelphia Phillies as an outfielder for his power at the plate and lightning-fast legs. Scott was in the minors for two years before deciding he would never make it to the majors and changed careers. Dan was still with the Phillies, now with their AAA team—the Lehigh Valley IronPigs—with hopes for a permanent position in major league baseball. He had been called up twice to the majors for a few days to replace an injured Philly centerfielder, only to be sent down again when the injured player returned. He remained determined to make it to the majors full time.

Dan and Scott had maintained contact over the years although they had not been able to spend much time together since their graduation. But Scott didn't think twice about who he would ask to be his best man. And he was delighted and honored that Dan had agreed. Opening day for the IronPigs was only a couple weeks away, and the team was at the height of the spring training season, but Dan gladly accepted. He was not able to leave until after the Thursday morning workout, but he put Scott's Savannah apartment address in his GPS, and once he got on the road, he made good time, stopping only for gas and coffee. Scott greeted him with a cold beer, and after a short conversation about the schedule of events, Dan was in bed and fast asleep.

Scott picked up his mother and sister from the airport shortly after noon and took them to the bed and breakfast where they would be staying until Monday. They would settle in and later take a stroll to Forsyth Park, a few blocks away. Scott planned to pick them up for dinner at the Library and introduce them to the Juri and Jaak.

He returned to his apartment to find Dan up with a fresh-made sandwich on a plate in front of him and a fresh pot of coffee on the small kitchen counter. Scott poured a cup and briefed Dan on where he had been and the plans for dinner that night.

"This is my first time as a best man," said Dan. "I got some help from a professional wedding director on my duties, and I've written them down." He pulled a folded sheet of paper from his pocket.

"I didn't know the best man had any duties, except to just be at the ceremony as 'best man.'"

"Well, my professional wedding director from Allentown says I have quite a few. So, this being the first time you've gotten married, and my first time as a best man, let me go over them and make sure we are on track."

Scott thought this was strange and began to laugh. "OK, let's go over your duties."

Dan looked at his notes. "Number one. Create the best man emergency kit. She said you never know what mishaps may occur on the morning of the wedding, so, as the Boy Scout motto goes: Be prepared! Bandages, tissues, and pain relievers. Spray deodorant. Stain remover, sewing kit, and even an extra pair of black socks. I've got that covered. In the trunk of my car."

"Great!" said Scott. "You never know when you'll need to pull out that deodorant and start spraying. Next duty?"

"Number two. Help the groom choose tux."

"No tuxes at this wedding. I've some nice suits. Most good enough for trials, maybe not good enough for my wedding. So especially for the wedding, I upgraded to a snappy blue pin stripe from Macy's. It'll work well in the courtroom after the wedding. So, what's your next duty?"

"Number three. Make sure tux, suspenders, tux shirt, tie, and shoes are ready."

"Not applicable," said Scott. "Next?"

"Number four. Plan and give the bachelor party."

"No duty there, Dan. Remember, this is a small, low-budget

wedding. I told you when I asked you to be the best man that there would be no rehearsal and no bachelor party."

"Yes, I know. I'm just checking off what the professional planner gave me. So next is number five. Organize groomsmen's fittings and make sure the groomsmen are wearing their boutonnieres."

"Again, not applicable. No groomsmen. And boutonnieres are covered. Jennifer says the caterer insisted on providing them for the groom, the best man, father of the bride, and mothers of the bride and groom. And grandparents, but there are no grandparents. I guess caterer has close connections to florists and gets a good discount. Good PR. Not only that, I had planned to select Jennifer's corsage, but she says her father insists that he provide her corsage. That was fine with me. She's his only daughter—an only child—so this task is something special for him. Now, what's the next task?"

"Number six. Hold the wedding rings until the ring exchange. If there is no ring bearer, the best man may be responsible for holding the wedding bands until the ring exchange portion of the ceremony. Be aware of where the rings are at all times and keep them in a safe place, like your inner jacket pocket. Check in advance that your pocket doesn't have a hole in it!" Dan noted that Scott's jaw went slack, and his eyes widened as he read.

"Ah, man, I've screwed up. I don't have the rings!" Scott's face was in a grimace. "They are still at the jeweler, being sized. I was to pick them up yesterday. I had a bunch of stuff come up and didn't get away from the office until after 6:00. It just slipped my mind. I can't believe this."

"No problem—your best man to the rescue. Let's go in my car; you can give directions. I need to get familiar with the traffic and streets."

"Good," replied Scott. "I think they're open until 5:00. We have time."

They walked out and down the stairs and across the driveway to where Dan's car was parked. As they were getting in, he asked, "Do you have the receipt for picking them up?"

Scott closed his eyes and let out a deep breath. "No! It's on my dresser." Scott moved quickly across the driveway and bounded up the stairs. He was smiling and shaking his head when he returned, holding the receipt from the jeweler in his hand and showing it to Dan. "Thanks for the reminder," he said.

"As the wedding director said, the best man does have duties. Glad to help."

The trip to the jeweler was successful, and they returned to Scott's apartment. Dan removed the suit coat he would be wearing for the wedding from a hang-up bag. With a smile on his face—and with exaggerated movements to get Scott's attention—he carefully checked the inside pocket for any holes. Signaling with a thumbs-up that he found none, he placed the two rings in his coat's inside pocket.

"Safe now in the care of the best man," he said with a grin.

CHAPTER TWENTY-FOUR
Friday, March 20

With Scott driving his rental car, he and Dan rode over to the bed and breakfast to pick up Scott's mother and his sister, Dianne, for dinner. Scott's mom was about five feet four inches tall, in her late fifties, still trim and attractive with short brown hair with just a touch of gray. She had a soft voice reflecting her many years as a librarian in the small Tennessee town where as a widow she raised Dianne and Scott. Dianne was a couple of inches taller, with long blond hair, bright blue eyes, in her late twenties. She had a beautiful smile that she displayed often and was trim and attractive like her mother. Scott was proud of both. He wanted to have dinner at the Library grill and introduce them to Juri and Jaak. His mother had heard Scott speak of both many times, and she was anxious to meet them.

The Library was busy as usual for a Friday night, but Juri saw them as soon as they walked through the entrance. He was behind the bar speaking to someone on his cell phone. With a broad smile, he waved them forward and quickly concluded his call. One end of the bar had a few customers, but the center portion was empty, and Scott and the others took their seats.

"Let me give a special welcome to the groom and his party," Juri said when they had settled in. Scott introduced each of them to Juri, adding that Juri was a longtime special friend and would be tending the bar at the wedding.

"Yes, I'll be tending the bar tomorrow, but let me take care of you now. Anything you want—and it's all on me. Special wedding gift for my good friend Scott Marino."

Soon the drinks were sitting before the two ladies, and mugs of beer were sliding across the bar top, landing, as intended, directly in front of Scott and Dan. When that was accomplished, Juri walked over to where they were seated. Scott placed a large envelope on the bar. He had brought it from his apartment and into the Library, unnoticed by Dan.

"For you, Juri."

Juri began to open the envelope. He removed an eight by ten colored photo and placed it on the bar. Juri picked it up, looked carefully at it for a long moment and then with a broad smile, held it up for everyone to see. It was a photo of Dan in his Philadelphia Phillies uniform made during his first trip to the majors. White uniform with bright red letters, "Phillies," across the front.

Dan grinned. "Where did you get that, Scott? I don't even have that photo."

"I have my sources," Scott responded, as he reached in his pocket for a pen. "I want you to sign and date it. 'To Juri'—spelled J-U-R-I—'from your Philly friend.'" Scott turned to face Juri. "Dan is with Philadelphia's triple-A team. Centerfielder. Called up to the majors a couple of times, so he's an authentic major leaguer, making it big time with the Phillies. He can give you some hint of what Atlanta can expect from the Phillies this season."

"Well, they won fourteen out of eighteen from us last year on their way to winning the World Series. They are good, every year. I expect they'll eat our lunch again."

"Maybe not. We've had our share of injuries. Cole Hamels, our best starting pitcher, left camp Monday with an elbow problem. He was to pitch for our opener April 5. And second baseman Chase Utley had hip surgery over the winter. Don't know how that's going to play out."

"Yeah, those injuries can hurt—no pun intended," said Juri.

"I think the Braves were lucky. Few injuries last year, but I worry about Chipper Jones. He's thirty-six years old, you know."

"But he won the league batting title last year—somewhere in the three-sixties."

Scott broke in. He knew both Juri and Dan were having fun talking baseball, but he had brought his mom and sister for dinner. "We're going into the grill for dinner. You guys can keep talking baseball." And they did.

Dan joined them about ten minutes later and had the pen Scott had given him for signing. "Here's your pen. Photo signed. Juri wanted me to add that it was signed at the Library. He said he would post it behind the bar."

"I'll have to see that," said Scott. "He's such a devoted Atlanta Braves fan."

They all ordered, and of course, the conversation focused on the upcoming wedding. Scott was giving a description of the wedding site, the Winery, when Jaak walked over to their table. Scott immediately stood to shake Jaak's hand.

Smiling broadly, he introduced Jaak, explaining their longtime relationship and how Jaak had been such a help to him on so many occasions. His mom and sister had heard quite a bit about Jaak over the years, and they were delighted to meet him.

They conversed for a few minutes, and as Jaak was leaving, he looked directly at Scott's mom. "Mrs. Marino, I want to congratulate you on raising your son to become such a fine young man in all respects. I don't have a son, but should I have one, I would feel blessed if he had the character of your son. I know you are proud of him, and I'm proud to call him a special friend. And he has chosen a beautiful and special young lady to be his bride. They are a beautiful couple, and I look forward to being present tomorrow when they exchange their vows." He then turned to the others. "It was my pleasure to have met you, and I look forward to seeing you again tomorrow." As he turned and walked away, they were all smiling, but the broadest smile was on Scott's mom's face.

On the way out of the Library, Scott looked over at the bar. Juri was no longer there, but he thought he noted something new on the wall behind the bar. He walked over for a closer look. Dan's photo had been attached. A photo of a Philly player was not something Scott would have ever expected at Juri's bar. But Juri had met a genuine major league baseball player and was quite proud of it. And being the ever-loyal Braves fan he was, the photo was carefully placed at least twelve inches *under* the one of Scott in his Braves uniform and the autographed photo of Bobby Cox.

CHAPTER TWENTY-FIVE

Saturday, March 21

T he plan for Saturday afternoon was for both Dan and Scott to drive their cars to the wedding, with Scott picking up his mom and sister on the way. The Winery was located in a remote location out on Betz Creek on Wilmington Island. It wasn't easy to give directions, so Dan would just follow Scott in Scott's rental car. Earlier Dan had asked Scott about his Camaro.

"Do you still have your pride and joy, your old Z28?"

"I do, but I have it in storage. I'm driving a Malibu now. Nice to have a bit more room." All of that was true, and he did not elaborate. It seemed a satisfactory answer to Dan's question, and Dan did not inquire further. Scott was not about to tell him of his getaway plans. Dan had a prankster reputation from his college days, and that would be a valuable bit of intelligence if Dan had plans for decorating Scott's getaway car. He didn't need to know anything further.

Scott, with his mom and sister, arrived at the Winery at 4:15 p.m., with Dan right behind. The parking lot had only a few cars. Scott recognized one that appeared to be Jennifer's dad's car. Also, the caterer's large van was parked close to the entrance, along with a van from the Library with the bar supplies. The Winery was a large open pavilion, with a stage and several small dressing rooms for musicians and other performers who appeared there. Early in the wedding planning, Jennifer had set aside one for her and her family and another for Scott and his family. But that did not mean they were adhering to the old superstition that it was bad luck for the couple to see each other on the day of the wedding before the ceremony. In fact, they had arranged for the wedding photographer to arrive in time to take their portraits together before the ceremony. The private rooms were to accommodate last-minute dressing details.

Jennifer was with her mom, near the outside railing, overlooking the broad stretch of saltwater marshes that surrounded the Winery on three sides. She was in her wedding dress, wearing a beautiful corsage of white roses on her wrist. She turned and saw Scott. Smiles appeared on the faces of both. Scott walked quickly toward her and they embraced as Scott whispered in her ear, "I love you, and you are so beautiful." Nearby was the ever-alert photographer, and he captured the scene with his camera.

Nicole Chapman, Jennifer's only bridesmaid, was near the stage area but joined the group when she saw Scott. Scott introduced his mother and sister—and Dan, noting that he had driven over 700 miles from Pennsylvania on Thursday for this special occasion. Jennifer's mom retrieved the boutonnieres from the caterer for Scott and Dan and pinned them on. She also had one for Scott's mom. Then the photographer went into action, giving directions and snapping photos of all participants, individually, in groups, and especially of the bride and groom together.

As soon as there was a break in the photography activity, Scott looked for the bar setup, which was on the far side of the pavilion, near the caterer's food table. It was complete and ready for business. There was also a table where Juri had set up his music system, which was connected to the Winery's speakers. Both Juri and Jaak were seated nearby.

"Thanks, Jaak, thanks Juri. So glad you are here. Jennifer and I appreciate all you have done for us."

"Glad to be here, glad to help," said Jaak. "I guess we're a bit early. I understood the ceremony was set for 5:00."

"It *is* set for 5:00," said Scott, who then held his hand out to check the time. His watch showed the time was 4:50 p.m. He looked at the portion of the pavilion that had been prepared for the ceremony. There was a white wooden arch, covered with flowers, located where their wedding vows would be exchanged. Although the flowers were artificial, they looked quite real. It was a permanent and rather expensive fixture at the Winery, which often hosted weddings. A hundred chairs had been placed for the guests to view the ceremony. Scott noted with concern that there were only about a half-dozen guests seated. He recognized three friends from the District Attorney's Office and two young women whom he recognized as Jennifer's classmates from Savannah Law. Jaak's wife, Lois, was seated in midrow, just a few rows back from the ceremonial area.

"I'm not experienced in this, Jaak, but I would have expected most of the guests to be here by now. I don't think we are going to be able to start at 5:00."

"They may be having trouble finding the Winery, way out here in the marshes," replied Jaak.

"I prepared a detailed map with directions, and Jennifer sent it to everyone."

"She even sent me one," added Juri. "I didn't use it; I knew the way. But it was accurate. They couldn't get lost."

"Well, we'll just wait until they get here," said Scott. "There could have been an accident blocking the road. I'll go check-in with Pastor Bacon—let him know there's going to be a delay." And at that moment, Scott realized he had not seen the pastor. He looked across the pavilion. The only people visible were the few seated guests and the members of the catering crew.

He walked over to the lady who appeared in charge of the catering. They exchanged greetings, and Scott asked if she had seen the pastor. The answer was "no."

Jennifer and her parents had gone to the reserved room to wait. Scott went to find them and inform them of the delay. He had a stressed look on his face when he entered the room where they were waiting. It was just a few minutes before 5:00 p.m.

"Very few of the guests have arrived," said Scott, "so I think we should delay the ceremony a while. And I haven't seen Pastor Bacon. Have you?"

"No," replied Jennifer. "I assumed he was with you."

"Maybe he hasn't arrived yet. That really surprises me. He said he knew exactly where the Winery was, said he had been here. And the time was always 5:00, never changed. He even suggested the time. I'll go see if I can find him. I know he drives a blue MINI Cooper. I can see the entire parking lot from up here. His MINI is easy to spot."

Scott walked out on the floor of the pavilion. It was on pilings about fifteen feet up from ground level. He could survey not only the parking lot but also see far down the narrow two-lane road that twisted and turned through the marshes to the pavilion. The MINI wasn't in the parking lot, and he could see no incoming traffic on the road. But Scott also saw that the parking lot was still sparsely occupied. Besides the two vans that brought the bar supplies and catered food, there were only eight vehicles, and that was counting his and Dan's. He went over to the bar, where Jaak and Juri were seated.

"Jaak, the pastor is not here, and most of the guests who said they would be coming haven't arrived. There must be a traffic problem, maybe an accident blocking the road."

"I can check that out; I have the Chatham County Sheriff's Office number on my cell. Give me a moment."

Jaak pulled his phone from his pocket. He walked to the railing to make sure he had a clear connection and made the call. He returned quickly with his results.

"I spoke with a deputy. He said he would have to do some checking and would call me back as soon as he found out."

"I'm going to update Jennifer and her family. And my mom. I'm sure they're all wondering what's going on."

Scott found his mom and sister, together with Dan and the photographer, in their room. Dan and the photographer were in a lively discussion about the upcoming baseball season. Scott told them the situation but could offer no explanation. The pastor and the guests just haven't arrived. He then went to the room where Jennifer, her parents, and Nicole were waiting. He explained that the guests had not arrived and neither had Pastor Bacon.

"I think I have the pastor's phone number in my cell. I'm going to call him."

Scott pulled his cell from his pocket and called. He got the church's answer machine, giving the times for Sunday services, youth group meetings, and choir practice on Wednesday night. But no number for contacting the pastor late Saturday afternoon. Scott realized that although he had spoken with the pastor several times, it was never on the pastor's cell phone or home phone, and he did not have either of those phone numbers.

"Jennifer, would you have the pastor's cell or home phone?" Scott asked.

"No—always contacted him at the church office."

"Do you know any neighbors or close friends?"

Jennifer paused and seemed to be thinking. But the answer was "no."

Scott looked at his watch. It was 5:30 p.m. He went out to the pavilion rail and looked again at the parking lot. He saw that no additional vehicles had arrived. He thought the half-dozen guests that had been seated for almost an hour should be advised of the situation. On the way to speak to them, he passed by the bar where Jaak and Juri were seated.

"I just got a response from the sheriff's office. No accidents or road closings out this way," Jaak informed him.

Scott was visibly stressed. This was to be the most important and happiest day of his life. And it had arrived on a perfect spring day, with his mother and sister flying in from Tennessee to be present when he exchanged vows with the most beautiful and bright young lady he had ever known. How could this wedding catastrophe happen? By now the ceremony should have been concluded and the guests should have been serving themselves at the caterer's table or lined up at the bar, giving Juri their drink orders. Or seated at one of the numerous tables on the far side of the pavilion enjoying their dinner and drinks, laughing and joining in the celebration. Instead, he looked over at the tables filled with food, and a table holding a beautiful, white, three-tiered wedding cake. But where were the guests who had been invited to celebrate this special occasion with them?

There were exactly six. They were still seated among the 100 folding chairs that had been set up to accommodate the expected guests. Scott walked over to where they were seated to explain that the wedding was being delayed to await the late arrivals. They smiled as if they understood. Scott was pleased they had no questions, as he had no answers. He walked back to the bar area, perhaps hoping that Jaak had a suggestion. Could or should they just proceed with the ceremony? But he then remembered that there was no official or pastor present to hear their vows. The only words of comfort Jaak or Juri could utter was the guests surely will be arriving soon. But Scott knew better. He took a seat in a chair beside Jaak. The stress of the situation increased by the minute as not a single guest had arrived since Scott last looked at the parking lot.

Suddenly, Scott heard footsteps and an excited voice behind him. He stood and turned to see Joy White, who had been among the early arrivals. She had a cell phone in her hand.

"Scott! You've got to read this text on my phone. I had my phone alert off since last night and hadn't seen this message until a few minutes ago." She handed the phone to Scott. She was breathing heavily, her eyes were wide, and she was biting her lower lip.

Scott took the phone and read the message to himself. Then he slowly turned his head and looked off into a distant view of the salt marshes. He said nothing. After a long moment, he handed the phone to Jaak, directing him to the text message on the phone. The message read:

"This is a very personal message. Jennifer and Scott have postponed their marriage. I ask that you do not discuss this with anyone. Jennifer wanted me to contact you now, and she will contact you on Sunday with an explanation. I am making this request to all invited guests to honor her privacy. Please, no gossip. Should anyone contact you about this, please remind them of our request for the utmost privacy. Thank you. Mrs. Patrick Stone (Jennifer's mother)"

Jaak read the message silently, then handed the phone to Juri. Jaak looked directly at Scott and said, "I'm sorry, Scott. Someone has played a terrible joke on you and Jennifer. Do you know anyone who would do this—or any reason a person would do this? Obviously, someone had a complete guest list and phone numbers."

Scott turned and lowered his head for a long moment before replying. "We used an electronic service for our invitations. The way we had it set up, everyone invited could view all names on the guest list. We did this so they could share rides. But phone numbers and email addresses weren't viewable. Pastor Bacon was not on the guest list, but whoever planned and executed this apparently got to him also."

Scott looked around the pavilion and saw all the food on the table that would be wasted and the beautiful tiered wedding cake that remained on the small table, still uncut. The day that was to be the happiest day of his life had turned into the saddest day of his life. He turned and again looked off into the distant marshes. He shook his head slowly from side to side and for a long moment, he remained silent. Then in an anguished voice, he said, to no one in particular, "All that food, bought and paid for, now just going to waste."

"No Scott, it will not go to waste," said Jaak. "It will be enjoyed at your wedding tomorrow afternoon at the Library if you agree. We have refrigeration to keep the food overnight, and as you know, the Library is closed on Sundays. We have plenty of room, dance floor, nice professionally stocked bar. We'll open the Library for you and Jennifer and have a spectacular wedding to remember—just a day late. The Library is yours tomorrow, any time, if you want it."

As what Jaak was telling him was sinking in, Scott began to smile.

"If we want it? Of course, we want it, Jaak. That's perfect. Let me go speak with Jennifer. I'll be right back."

Jennifer and her family and her bridesmaid were still in the assigned room. Scott explained the text message that Joy White had received early in the morning, but had just discovered, and the offer from Jaak to have the wedding at the Library the next day. Everyone in the room was shocked by the news of the deceitfulness. But the answer was immediate. *Yes!*

"We'll have to contact Pastor Bacon and see when he's available," said Jennifer, a faint smile finally replacing the sadness her face had shown since she first realized their wedding plans had gone astray.

"We don't have any time to spare," said Scott. "We have to get the word out immediately about the hoax and let the guests know the time and place as soon as possible. I think we should set it at 5:00, just as we had planned for today. If Pastor Bacon isn't available, I'm sure I can find a judge or a justice of the peace who will perform the ceremony."

"Scott is right," said Jennifer's dad. "Let's do it, 5:00, at the Library. What a wonderful friend you have in Jaak, Scott. Incredible—he immediately saw and offered a solution to such an overwhelming problem. But can you think of who would have pulled such a mean, atrocious trick on you and Jennifer?"

"It's really beyond my comprehension now, Patrick. I know there's evil in this world, but to sabotage a wedding . . ." Scott stopped in mid-sentence. "Right now, I need to go tell Jaak and Juri that we would be honored to have the ceremony at the Library." And with that, Scott departed.

He went immediately to assure Jaak that Jennifer accepted his offer with delight and many thanks. Juri had already loaded most of the bar supplies and the portable bar into his van. Scott looked where the six guests had been and noted they were still there. He told them of the plans for Sunday, and they all promised to be present. He then went to the room where his mom, sister, and best man were waiting. They listened attentively as Scott told them of the text message and Jaak's offer to host the wedding on Sunday. Their faces reflected their disappointment as well as their bewilderment. The first to speak was his best man.

"So, Scott, the wedding is now on track, now we need to get the honeymoon on track. You told me you would be going to The Lodge on St. Simons Island. I'll contact them and tell them you won't be arriving until tomorrow."

"I have their number on my cell phone." Scott pulled his phone from his coat pocket and located the number. "Just use my phone, Dan." Scott handed the phone to Dan, and Dan soon had the front desk at The Lodge. Dan turned on the phone speaker for Scott to hear.

"I'm calling to cancel the reservation for today for Scott Marino, but keep the remaining days of the reservation."

"Just a moment, let me look that up," was the response from the man at the desk. In a few moments, he returned to the phone. "That reservation has already been canceled. Yesterday, by phone, according to the note here."

"That's strange. Mr. Marino did not make that cancelation. But that's OK, he'll be there tomorrow night."

"Sir, we have no rooms for tomorrow. He released his room, and it has been reserved for another party."

Dan's face flushed, and in an angry voice he told the man at the desk that Scott Marino would be there tomorrow, and the hotel would be expected to provide him a room for his honeymoon. Dan returned the phone to Scott and said, "Your best man will follow up on this in the morning. You'll be staying at the Lodge on St. Simons Island for your honeymoon. Trust me."

Scott smiled, his first smile since the wedding debacle. "Whoever sabotaged our wedding tried to do the same for the honeymoon. But how on earth did they get information about where we were going? We didn't try to keep it a secret, but it wasn't common knowledge to my friends or Jennifer's." Scott's voice was expressing more bewilderment than anger. "Well, nothing we can do about it now. Let's go out and see how the transfer of food is going. Maybe they need some help."

As he walked out of the room, he saw the lady in charge of catering heading his way. She asked Scott if he knew where Mr. or Mrs. Stone was located. Scott took her to the room where he last saw them. They were still there, getting ready to depart. She handed Patrick Stone an invoice.

"This is for the fifty percent additional food Mrs. Stone ordered Friday."

Patrick looked surprised and turned to his wife, as the caterer continued. "We were able to get it from our wholesale supplier. I told them it was for a wedding reception, and they made a special effort to get it for us just in time."

Mrs. Stone spoke up. "I did not call for additional food. You say you received a call Friday afternoon?"

"Yes, the caller said it was for the wedding the following day at the Winery."

"No, no. There's been a mistake."

"But I took the call myself. It was a female voice, and she identified herself as Mrs. Patrick Stone, mother of the bride."

"But I did not call."

Patrick took the invoice from the caterer's hand, examined it, and took a deep sigh. "I think I know what this is—just another demonic act by the devil who wrecked the wedding. Not the fault of anyone here. I'll take care of this, but give us a few days. This has been a stressful day, and I don't want to think about it now. But I assure you that you will get paid."

"Mr. Stone," the caterer replied. "I'm fully aware of all that happened this afternoon. Your daughter's wedding, ruined. Let me have that invoice. I'm going to speak to the owner. I'll explain what occurred, and I'll suggest she charge only what the wholesaler charged us. And I assure you that my team will be at the Library tomorrow to assist with the food. And there will be no additional charge for that."

Patrick returned the invoice back to the lady. "Thanks," he said, and then turning to others, added, "now let's leave this miserable place and forget about this cruel trick. We need to get those corrected invitations out." He then reached for his daughter and gave her a warm embrace. "Tomorrow," he said, "is a new day, and we are going to have a beautiful wedding for a beautiful bride!"

Jennifer wiped away a tear and smiled.

CHAPTER TWENTY-SIX
Saturday, March 21

J essica had accepted a date with Anderson McDowell as a continu-
ation of her "assignment." It wasn't an awful date; she had had
worse. McDowell had taken her to the same restaurant for dinner,
the Loca Luna. They saw a couple they had met there during their
previous visit—Paul Acosta and Sheri Schauer. Paul waived them
over, and the four of them shared a table.

Just as Jessica and Andy were sitting down, Jessica's phone
buzzed. She reached in her purse, pulled it out, and immediately saw
it was a text message from her aunt. She quickly read it and replaced
the phone into her purse.

"Text from my aunt," she said. "She changed the number on our
home alarm system and wanted to make sure I had it. She told me
this morning that she had changed it, but being the worrier she is,
just wanted to make sure I had it."

"That's neat," said Paul. "I have a primitive phone—takes and
makes phone calls, that's it. No email, no text. But I'm upgrading it
this coming week to the new iPhone."

"You will love it," replied Jessica. "I have a running dialogue with
my Aunt about her real estate business. I'm still an associate in the
firm, and she keeps me informed with text messages. I can look up
all the text messages she's sent to me over the past couple of weeks,
and there they are, all still on my phone. And I better call her now

and let her know I got her message. As I said, she's a worrier." Jessica removed her phone from her purse and began dialing.

The conversation was brief. "That was interesting," said Andy, as she finished the conversation.

"You say it was 'interesting?'" responded Jessica with a quizzical look.

"Not the conversation, but you just picked up your phone and tapped in her phone number without entering any code to unlock it."

"That's because I have it programmed for immediate access—for safety reasons. My aunt's been in the real estate sales business for a long time. She says it can get a bit creepy, visiting unoccupied homes alone with a client that you've just met and know little about. She insisted that I have the phone programmed for immediate access—no passcode required."

Paul was an experienced and quite talented Latin dancer; Sheri was not quite there yet. Several times during the evening, Paul invited Jessica to dance with him, and Andy looked on approvingly. After each dance with Paul, Jessica would invite Andy out on the dance floor, give him a few tips, and applaud his progress. The dinner was fine, and the foursome had a lively conversation about the Loco Luna, Atlanta, Latin dances and travel. This was the easy and pleasant part of the date.

Shortly after 9:00 p.m., Jessica's phone beeped with a text message. She lifted the phone from her purse and immediately saw the message she had hoped she would be receiving that evening. It read:

"Wedding of Jennifer and Scott was postponed today for unexpected circumstances beyond the control of anyone. The wedding will take place tomorrow, Sunday, March 22, 2009. Please join us at 5:00 p.m. at the Library Bar and Grill, 1936 McCain Street, Savannah (adjacent to Savannah College of Law) as Jennifer and Scott exchange their vows. Dinner and dancing to follow."

Beyond the control of anyone? Ha! Not exactly, Jessica mused as she beamed and placed the phone back in her purse.

"You're smiling. Some pleasant news?" asked Andy.

"You might say that," replied Jessica, as the smile broadened.

"Well, I did say that. Why don't you share your good news?"

"Oh, it's just me reflecting on my unbridled rancorous conduct."

"Your what?!"

"Oh, just forget it. Time to get back on the dance floor."

She grabbed Andy's hand and led him out as the band began to play "La Tortura," one of Jessica's favorites. She continued to smile as they danced.

Jessica enjoyed the evening with Andy and their newfound friends. *Not a bad work assignment*, she thought. Afterward, just as Jessica expected, Andy stopped his car during the drive through nearby Piedmont Park, parking just off the road near the lake. There, Andy made a move on Jessica, as she had expected. He quickly slid over and embraced her. She did not resist initially. They kissed, and she allowed his hands to roam over her breasts briefly but stopped him when he tried to become more intimate.

"Andy, no, not now. This just isn't the place and I need more time. You do understand, don't you? I don't want you to remember me as some loose woman who you soon became bored with."

Andy pulled away from her quickly. "Of course, I understand—and I would never think of you as 'loose,' as you use that word, or ever become bored with you. It's just that you are so beautiful and .. . I . . . I . . . I want . . ." He stopped. Then he said softly, "I'm sorry."

"No need to feel sorry. I enjoy these moments too. But it's just too early in our relationship. Just a few more weeks. Let's get that trial over with. I'm going to ask Colosimo if I can go with the team to Savannah. And hopefully, we can stay a day or two afterward to celebrate—just the two of us. Tom and the boss can depart for Atlanta. You and I can depart for the hotel if you are still interested."

Andy smiled. "I'll wait, but it won't be easy."

"The best things in life are never easy," Jessica said, returning his smile and running her fingers gently through his hair.

Jessica arrived home just a little before midnight. She was tired but wanted to get a text message off to Colosimo before retiring. She found her cell phone and began texting.

> "Out with Andy tonight—he didn't mention
> trial. He's holding steady. I promised him
> an all-nighter at the Hyatt after the trial
> (he believes it!). That will keep him running
> the bases—he's about to 2nd! Ha Ha.
> This is a fun job. Nice dinner once a week.
> PS: Sent in my application for admission to
> Adam Lansky. Do your magic."

CHAPTER TWENTY-SEVEN

Sunday, March 22

Jaak and Juri were up early Sunday morning to ensure that the Library was perfect for the wedding scheduled there at 5:00 p.m. Juri would be in charge of beverages and assisting the catering crew in preparing—again—the food that had been stored overnight in the Library's refrigeration units. The beverages would be served from the bar, so that was already taken care of. Jaak would take charge of setting up the chairs for the wedding guests and the tables for the dinner to follow. Saturday night had been a busy night at the Library, and Jaak wanted to make sure it was clean and orderly well in advance of the wedding. He did not want to call any of his employees to come in on their day off, so he was prepared to sweep, mop, and dust as needed. Over the years of owning and managing two Savannah bars, he had frequently performed such work, and he was good at it. He did plan to call a couple of the waitresses to see if they could come in later to help out with the wedding dinner.

Jaak recalled the white arched arbor that was to be the backdrop for the wedding ceremony at the Winery. He checked to see if Home Depot on Abercorn was open. It was not yet—but it would be open at 8:00 a.m. And when it opened, Jaak was parked outside the garden shop in his van. He quickly found what he was looking for. In the garden shop was a white arched wooden arbor—seven feet high and four feet wide—assembled and ready for pickup. At first, he thought he would have to disassemble it to move it, but with just a little help from a Home Depot worker, he was able to load it into his van just as it was. Soon after returning to the Library and setting up the arched arbor, the building was beginning to take on an appropriate appearance for a small wedding. Jaak called his wife, Lois, and they made plans to have the arbor decorated with fresh flowers from their front and back yards. Like many Savannah homes, Jaak and Lois's home was surrounded by an array of beautiful spring flowers, especially camellias, azaleas, and Lois's specialty, gerberas. By midafternoon the wedding arbor at the Library would be beautifully decorated with fresh pink and white flowers, the skilled handiwork of Lois.

Scott did not sleep well Saturday night. He was up early, quickly dressed in shorts and athletic shoes and went for a run on some of Savannah's narrow one-way streets. Dan was sleeping soundly when he left. The streets were mostly empty of vehicles, and he kept a steady pace for the two-mile jog to Forsyth Park. Besides a homeless man still sleeping on a couple of blankets under some trees about twenty yards south of the fountain, it seemed that Scott had the park all to himself. He sat on a wooden bench and gazed at the 150-year-old fountain. It was still under the spell of one of Savannah's St. Patrick's Day celebrations—the water flowing from the fountain was bright green.

The green water initially surprised Scott although it should not have. He was well aware that it was customary on the Friday before St. Patrick's Day for green dye to be poured into the water at the Forsyth Park fountain. The Triton figures in the lower basin were spouting bright green water from the horn-like instruments they held in their mouths, while the upper basin maintained a showery green spray all around its perimeter. The Friday dye-pouring event marked the beginning of Savannah's St. Patrick's Day celebrations, which included a parade that rated among the largest St. Patrick's Day parades in the nation. Each year since his arrival in Savannah as a law student, Scott had viewed the parade, and a couple of times had attended the Greening of the Fountain ceremony in Forsyth Park. All nine of the fountains in Savannah's Historic District received the dye, but Forsyth Park's fountain ceremony was the featured event. There, the dye was poured into the water by the Grand Marshall of the parade which would follow on St. Patrick's Day. Scott's work at the office and the preparations for the wedding had occupied his mind in recent days, and he had completely forgotten about the Greening of the Fountains. And though he had missed Friday's ceremony, he was pleased to be able to view the transformed fountain with its green water spewing out from the horns of the Triton figures. It would be replaced with clear water in a day or two. He sat resting from his jog, reminiscing the times he and Jennifer had strolled the park hand in hand in the early evenings.

But the events of the previous day played again and again in his mind—the ruined wedding and the sadness he saw in Jennifer's eyes, as she tried to maintain a smile through the afternoon, even after the shock of realizing the wedding would not take place as they had so carefully planned and expected. He knew the sadness was also shared by Jennifer's parents and his mother, all of whom had shared the initial excitement of a day promising such joy but which ended in such deep disappointment and pain. For a few moments, the beauty of the park, with the moss-draped live oaks and the lush greenery surrounding him in all directions gave him some respite from the sadness he felt as images of the events at the Winery raced through his mind. He longed to be with Jennifer, but that would have to wait. She had left the Winery with her parents, to spend Saturday night at their home in Hilton Head. He did not even have his cell phone with him to call.

He rested for a few more minutes, watching the swirling green water from the fountain and thinking of the rescheduled wedding at the library later that afternoon. He still had his Camaro packed and prepared for a honeymoon trip, but where that would be, he did not know. The reservations for the Lodge at St. Simons Island had been canceled, according to the clerk when Dan called from the Winery. He was to pick up his mother and sister from their bed and breakfast at 4:00. Juri was making his office at the Library available for Scott's family before the ceremony. Jaak, whose office was larger, was making his office available for Jennifer and her family. Scott reflected on how lucky he and Jennifer were to have such friends. He would find a way to repay them someday for this special friendship.

It was past Scott's usual breakfast time. He looked at his watch: 8:45 a.m. His favorite breakfast restaurant, Clary's Café, opened at 8:00 a.m., and it was only a few blocks away on Abercorn. He jogged over quickly. For all of the past week, breakfast had been coffee and cold cereal, but this morning he would have coffee and one of Clary's famous omelets. When his meal arrived, he was able to forget the events of Saturday and for a few minutes fully enjoy this beautiful Sunday morning.

Later, when he arrived at his apartment, Dan was up, enjoying a fresh cup of coffee.

"Sorry for being such a lousy host, Dan. But I just had to go for a run. And a hot breakfast. Get your shoes on, and I'll take you to Clary's Café. You'll love it!"

"I'm not a breakfast guy, Scott. Black coffee and toast, which I was able to find in your completely disorganized kitchen, is all I need. And I have some news."

"Good or bad?"

"Good. The Best Man is not permitted to bring bad news. Your honeymoon site remains the same. All reserved. They'll be expecting you at The Lodge on St. Simons Island tonight, just as you had planned."

Scott smiled broadly, hoping he had heard correctly. "That's incredible, Dan. How did you do that?"

"You were in professional baseball for how many years? Two? Well, it's been my life now for seven years. As you know, minor leagues entirely, except for those call-ups to the Phillies as an emergency replacement. So, I've lived spring until fall in hotels in a dozen or so different cities, some good, some bad. Check in for two or three days, then check out for the next city, different hotel. Often three different hotels in a week. Can't do that for seven years without getting to know a bit how they work. So, you're back on for the Lodge—and how I did it is not important—just consider it done."

"Good enough—I won't ask for details. Just hope there wasn't a lot of violence involved. Or is that the secret?" They both laughed.

"I'm going to drive over to the Library and see if Jaak and Juri need help," said Scott. "Put your shoes on and come along." Scott knew they did not need his help, but he was anxious to call Jennifer and wanted to be able to give her an update on their new wedding site and the ongoing preparation. He also wanted to know if Jennifer had made contact with Pastor Bacon and if he would be available to officiate at the rescheduled wedding. He recalled he had volunteered to find a substitute—a judge or magistrate if Pastor Bacon was unavailable. He hadn't really given that possibility much thought, and time was getting short.

He arrived at the Library to see both Jaak and Juri standing by the arched arbor. One of the Library's assistant bartenders, Phil, who Scott recognized from his many visits, was running a vacuum cleaner over by a rear exit. Lois was busy decorating the arbor with the fresh flowers from her yards. She wasn't finished, but Scott quickly saw it was going to be beautiful. He surveyed the interior of the Library and saw the spacious hall had already been arranged as a mini-chapel, with rows of chairs facing the arbor where the ceremony would be held. All beer and other advertisement had been removed. The dozens of bottles usually seen stacked high on shelves behind the bar had also been removed. Even the photos of Scott and Dan in their baseball uniforms had been taken down.

Scott looked at Jake and Juri. "This is spectacular! Jennifer will love it. I'm going to call her with an update, but I'll let the flowered trellis be a surprise. So, please excuse me while I call her. Meanwhile, put Dan to work."

Dan rubbed his palms together. "Yep, I'm ready for the heavy lifting!"

Scott stepped outside to make his call. At that moment, he saw Bill Baldwin walking up the steps.

"Morning, Scott. Thought you guys may need some help getting ready for that five o'clock crowd."

"Good morning, Bill. Jaak and Juri seem to be getting it in order, but maybe they could indeed use a hand."

"How about you and Jennifer? I saw you had a photographer on hand yesterday. Is he coming back?"

"No, he had another engagement for today."

"Then I'm your man! I've got a new Nikon D3. I would be pleased to do it. Say the word and I'll be here."

"The only word I can think of right now is 'thanks.' I know Jennifer will be more than pleased. You are indeed a friend, Bill, if annoying at times, if you know what I mean." Scott laughed.

Bill returned the laugh. "I know. Annoy is my middle name. Part of a reporter's job. I'll be here at 4:00 so we can take some more prenuptial shots."

Scott made his call, and Jennifer answered immediately. Scott said, "Have I told you lately that I love you?"

"No. But you can tell me now."

"I love you! Let's get married!"

"When?"

"How about today—at 5:00."

Both laughed into their phones. Scott was pleased that she was in such good spirits, and he brought her up to date on the Library arrangements, carefully leaving out the beautiful arched arbor of flowers.

Scott asked, "Have you made contact with Pastor Bacon?"

"Oh, yes! And he'll be there to preside. He got a similar message the others got, about the wedding being postponed. But his message said that I was too upset to speak. You would be contacting him soon and, in the meantime, to 'please respect our privacy' or something like that. Claimed to be from my mother. So, he waited to hear from you. And unfortunately, my cell phone was the number he had for contacting either of us, so he was stymied on what he was to do. And I had only his church phone number. I called some of the folks I knew from church, but they didn't have his home phone either. This morning he decided he should contact me. He was shocked. And so apologetic. I tried to assure him he wasn't at fault, but he thinks he should have done more to check it out. Anyway, he says for sure, he'll be at the Library to conduct the ceremony. I'm really happy now; things are going to be fine."

"You bet. Better than fine. I love you so much, Jennifer." He paused then took a deep breath. "And I'll see you about 4:00 or so. We'll have some more photos to take. It will make a beautiful album. A 'before and after'!"

Scott walked back into the Library and saw Dan helping Juri move tables to an open area just behind the chairs that had been set for the wedding guests.

"We don't have enough chairs for both the ceremony and tables being set for dinner," said Jaak, "but it'll be easy to move the chairs to the tables after the ceremony. Dan and I will oversee that while Juri and Phil serve up the drinks. We'll have a table in the center for the bridal party and family. We have enough chairs for that table. The catering crew chief called earlier. They'll be over about 3:00 to begin getting the food ready. They'll serve from the tables in the restaurant." He pointed to the small restaurant at one end of the much larger hall where the wedding ceremony would take place.

"So as soon as the ceremony is over," Jaak said, "the guests can start serving their plates in the restaurant and then seat themselves at the tables. We'll have those chairs moved in plenty of time. You and the bridal party and family can move to the center table immediately after the ceremony. I think it's all going to work out fine."

Scott just smiled, slowly shaking his head. "Jaak, how am I ever going to be able to repay you?"

"Oh, that should be easy." Jaak's hand went to Scott's shoulder and rested there. He looked directly into Scott's eyes. "You know, Lois and I never had any children. Getting to know you and Jennifer over the last few years has given us a lot of pleasure that we might have missed. To repay us, you ask? Just continue to keep Jennifer happy. I know you two are deeply in love. Just keep that fire burning. That will make us both happy—payment enough."

Scott continued to smile. "Jaak, never doubt it. That's a promise easy to keep."

CHAPTER TWENTY-EIGHT
Sunday, March 22

B ill Baldwin returned to the Library with his Nikon D3, and by 5:00 p.m. had already taken enough photos to fill two wedding albums. Both Scott and Jennifer arrived a little after 4:00 p.m., and Scott transferred Jennifer's honeymoon suitcase to his rental car, which was parked in a reserved spot for a quick exit later. All but a few seats facing the arched arbor were occupied. Apparently, the "reinvited" guests had taken the delayed wedding in stride—a minor inconvenience. They were here to celebrate. The arbor was now beautifully decorated in bright flowers, fresh from Jaak and Lois's yard. Juri would be manning the disc player and audio system from its location next to the bar.

Scott and Jennifer's plans from the beginning were for this to be a small informal wedding, requiring no rehearsal. They did let the wedding party know the order in which each would walk down the aisle, but that was the extent of instructions. They had left the music selection to Juri, and he had informed all the participants that the processional would consist of two selections and to "just follow the music."

Juri was playing "Love Story" from Taylor Swift's recently released album, *Fearless*, when Scott and Pastor Bacon appeared and stood under the arbor. Instantly Juri switched the music to Mozart's Wedding March. And with that music playing, Scott's mother and sister, escorted by Best Man Dan, walked down and took their seats, front row, right side. Dan then took his place beside Scott. Moments later, Patrick Stone was escorting his wife down to her seat on the left front row, then returning by a side route to the back row for his next escort duty. Next down the aisle was the Maid of Honor, Nicole Chapman, who proceeded to her place on the left side of the arbor.

With everyone in place, Juri switched to the "Trumpet Voluntary," and the guests turned and stood to see Jennifer on the arm of her dad, smiling broadly and walking toward the ceremonial arbor.

Juri was vindicated. He had promised that it would all work out like it had been carefully rehearsed. He was right. For a reconstituted wedding—from one planned for a Saturday at a pavilion overlooking the salt marshes surrounding Savannah, to one twenty-four hours later at a neighborhood bar—it could not have gone more smoothly.

Scott looked at Jennifer, now standing right in front of him, with a smile directed only at him. She was the most beautiful woman he had ever seen, even more beautiful than the day he fell in love with her, which was the day they met. The ache of the previous day had vanished.

Pastor Bacon stepped forward and turned his head slowly, surveying his audience. He paused for a moment, then began in a strong but friendly voice.

"Let me extend to all of you a very special welcome. We are here today to share with Jennifer and Scott one of the most important moments in their lives. I have spent considerable time over the past month meeting with them and discussing the significance of this ceremony. During this time, I have learned that they met two and a half years ago at Savannah Law—just a block away from where we are now standing—and that their love and understanding of each other has grown and matured, and now they have decided to live their lives together as husband and wife. Marriage is the greatest of blessings but also one of awesome responsibilities. The cornerstone of a happy and lasting marriage is love. Let me read from Corinthians 1:13.

'Love is always patient and kind. It is never jealous. Love is never boastful or conceited, it is never rude or selfish, it does not take offense and is not resentful. Love takes no pleasure in other people's faults but delights in the truth. It is always ready to excuse, to trust, to hope. It is always ready to endure whatever comes. True love does not come to an end.'"

After a brief pause, Pastor Bacon looked directly at Scott. "Scott, do you take Jennifer for your lawful wedded wife, to love, honor, comfort, and cherish her from this day forward, forsaking all others, keeping only unto her for as long as you both shall live?"

"I do," answered Scott.

"Jennifer, do you take Scott for your lawful wedded husband, to love, honor, comfort, and cherish him from this day forward, forsaking all others, keeping only unto him for as long as you both shall live?"

"I do." Then, adding with a smile, "Scott, you had me at 'hello!'"

That line from *Jerry Maguire* brought laughs from many of the guests. Scott grinned and replied, "Jennifer, I think I'd miss you, even if we'd never met." It was a line from a different movie, *The Wedding Date*. This verbal exchange was not planned, but they had at times playfully repeated the lines to each other. Jennifer would later confirm that it wasn't planned but was just something she wanted to say at the moment and would never regret it.

Pastor Bacon smiled briefly at the unexpected comments and continued the ceremony with the ring exchange. Scott had expected Dan, to whom he had entrusted both rings, to dramatically but falsely pantomime that he had lost or forgotten them, an act both had observed during the wedding of one of their fraternity brothers. He didn't. The rings were quickly produced and ceremoniously placed on the fingers of the bridal couple.

"Inasmuch as you, Scott, and you, Jennifer, have pledged your faith each to the other in the presence of God, your family, and friends, by the authority vested in me by the State of Georgia, I now pronounce you both husband and wife. You may kiss the bride."

They kissed in a passionate embrace as the guests clapped loudly. Moments later, the Pastor turned to face the audience. "Honored guests and family members, it is my pleasure to present to you, Mr. and Mrs. Scott Marino."

Juri, still minding the disc and sound system, began playing the recessional music, and Scott and his bride began walking the aisle to the table that had been prepared for the bridal party. They were followed by Dan and Nicole, Jennifer's mom and dad, and Scott's mother and sister. Champagne and Champagne glasses were on the table. Scott turned and looked at the other tables. Champagne bottles were resting in small buckets and Champagne glasses were on each table. He was surprised. Champagne had not been included in their wedding budget. Unknown to Scott or Jennifer, Jennifer's dad had made arrangements with Jaak early that morning. He believed something extra was called for after the debacle at the Winery the previous afternoon. The Library rarely had orders for more than a bottle or two of Champagne, and Jaak did not have sufficient Champagne or Champagne glasses to fill such a request. But he placed a call to an old friend, the manager of the bar at the Hilton, explained the problem, and it was quickly solved.

Soon the guests had served their plates at the buffet, and Juri and his assistant, Phil, had filled all the drink orders. Soft dance music was being played through the Library's sound system, and most of the guests were now seated and joining in casual conversation. Dan stood and tapped on a tall glass with a fork, and the room quickly became quiet. When he saw that he had the attention of all the tables, he picked up the karaoke microphone that had been placed there by Juri, to be used as needed. Juri was observing and turned on the sound.

"At our table, we have a dependable . . . caring . . . sincere . . . honest . . . and a great man." He paused, looked around the room and smiled. "But enough about me!" He laughed along with the guests before continuing.

"I want to extend thanks to all of you for coming this afternoon to celebrate the wedding of Scott and Jennifer. Some of you I've met;

others I hope to meet. I'm Dan Koleos, fraternity brother and room-mate of Scott for our last three years at the University of Alabama. So, you see, I know him well, and despite that, we remain friends." Scott and those at his table laughed. Jennifer gave Scott a puzzled, somewhat amused, look.

"Scott and I took several classes together. One was a literature seminar, which to my surprise, I liked very much. I was particularly impressed with that guy named Robert Frost. Frost was a philosopher as well as a poet. He is quoted as saying, 'It's a funny thing that when a man hasn't anything on earth to worry about, he goes off and gets married.'" Laughter followed and Dan continued.

"Of course, Frost is better known as a poet, the author of 'The Road Not Taken' which we studied in our class for a couple of weeks. It was a really short poem—not sure why it took so long, but we did have a lot of jocks in the class." Laughter followed, and Scott smiled broadly.

"The poem was written in the first person, ending with that person wondering if the right choice had been made at some crossroad in that person's life. Scott will never have to wonder. He will always know he made the right choice—a beautiful and intelligent choice.

"Some wise person once said, 'Don't marry the person you think you can live with; marry only the person you think you can't live without.' Earlier this year, Scott called me and said he had found the girl he could not live without and asked that I be his best man at the wedding. I accepted, but I don't like the title, because the best man tonight is sitting at our table, next to his new bride."

Dan reached down and picked up his Champagne glass. "And now, ladies and gentlemen, may I ask you to rise and join me as I propose a toast to truly the best man, Scott, and to his beautiful bride, Jennifer, wishing this charming couple health and happiness. Jennifer and Scott!"

The room quickly was filled with voices, "To Jennifer and Scott." A soon as the guests were again seated, Scott took the microphone from Dan and stood.

"Thanks to all of you for coming this afternoon to help celebrate this occasion. I know many of you had other plans for this afternoon. So did I. So did Jennifer. But you did not have to be here; we did. So I add a very special thanks.

"I'm sure you are all aware by now of how we ended up with the wedding today, here, rather than yesterday out at the Winery. Initially, I was quite angry that a person or persons would attempt to destroy the joy of our wedding. Now, I feel very fortunate that they tried. They only accomplished a brief postponement. But it intensified the excitement and pleasure of our wedding today. For, you see, their action provided confirmation of the love and support of many friends who stepped forward to provide this beautiful venue on such short notice and make this an even more special day. Jaak and Juri and their helpers; the catering crew who volunteered to be here—on their own time; our substitute wedding photographer, Bill Baldwin; Jaak's wife Lois who today decorated the archway with flowers from her own yard; Pastor Bacon, who, this being a Sunday, already had a busy day; and my Best Man, Dan, who somehow got our honeymoon reservations restored after they had been maliciously canceled; and of course Jennifer's mom and dad, and my mom, all who have been so supportive all our lives and especially during the last twenty-four hours. You will have our eternal gratitude.

"This is a marriage of love which necessitates that this is a day of love. From the passage Pastor Bacon read at our ceremony, 'Love takes no pleasure in the faults of others. It remains ready to excuse, to trust, to hope.' So, to the person or persons who briefly delayed our marriage for whatever purpose or reason, from this day forward Jennifer and I offer our forgiveness. We refuse to seek revenge or even seek identity. You actually did us a great favor. And to all of you who have joined us today to celebrate the greatest day of our lives, we offer our sincerest thanks."

Scott took his seat while all others present stood and clapped. Jennifer pulled him close and gave him a kiss. The evening was off to a good start. Juri put on music for dancing. Scott and Jennifer stayed just long enough to receive personal congratulation from the guests.

They gave hugs or handshakes to all at their table and waived at the guests as they walked to the exit doors. Their first stop was at the auto rental agency to turn in the rental car and pick up Scott's 1984 Camaro. Next stop, The Lodge on St. Simons Island.

And just as Dan had promised, their reservation at The Lodge was still good!

CHAPTER TWENTY-NINE

Friday, March 27

The four days at The Lodge passed all too quickly. Mornings found them quietly lounging around the pool and at sunset, walking hand in hand on the beautiful sandy beach and listening to the lapping of the waves. They enjoyed horseback riding along a maritime forest trail, with a return route along the beach. And kayaking through Sea Island's salt marshes, enjoying the gentle sea breezes and the salt-mist sprays. The Saturday fiasco had robbed them of an extra day at the resort, but it did not diminish the excitement and joy of their honeymoon.

They returned Thursday afternoon, and Scott moved his clothes and personal articles into Jennifer's apartment. They planned to live there until the lease expired in the fall, then either renew or find another apartment. Friday afternoon they would go to the Library to thank Juri and Jaak for rescuing their wedding from the disaster on Saturday.

They arrived a little after 6:00 p.m. and found Juri behind the bar. His back was to them, and he was filling a drink order for some law students at a table near the back of the lounge. When he finished, he placed the drinks on a tray for the waitress to deliver. Then he turned and saw Scott and Jennifer sitting at his bar. A broad smile came quickly.

"Well, well. The newlyweds! What a nice surprise!" He asked

Jennifer for her order and quickly filled it. He didn't ask Scott for his order; he knew it. Scott's beer in a frosted mug was sent with a flourish down the bar, followed by Juri self-congratulating his great aim and pumping his fist.

"Welcome back," he said, as his fist-pumping ended and the smile continued. "I know the honeymoon was at the Lodge. Never been there myself but have heard it is spectacular—all kinds of activities. What did you find to do—I mean during daylight hours?" He grinned.

Scott told him about the kayaking, horseback riding, the beautiful beaches, and the extensive maritime forest surrounding the resort.

"Sounds like a great start to a happy marriage," responded Juri. "My wife and I were happy for 21 years." He paused and looked away for just a moment before continuing. "Then we got married." They all laughed, but at the same time, Scott and Jennifer gave him four thumbs down.

"Juri, I'm sure you have advice you can give me for keeping a marriage happy." Scott smiled, knowing it was a loaded question, one for which Juri would surely have a clever answer.

"Sure. The husband must remember the five most important words in a marriage."

"And that is . . .?" asked Scott with a grin.

"I apologize. You are right." They all laughed, but only Scott gave it two thumbs down.

"How about advice for the wife?" asked Jennifer, knowing she was likely next, whether she asked or not.

"Just remember, Jennifer, a good wife always forgives her husband when she's wrong." It took a moment, but soon all three were laughing.

Scott turned and surveyed the large room where they had shared their marriage vows on the past Sunday. "We came to express our thanks to both you and Jaak for all the work you did to get our wedding ceremony back on schedule. But I haven't seen Jaak anywhere. Is he in his office?"

"No, he stepped out for some personal business. Said he would be gone for about an hour. He should be back soon."

"We'll wait. I know he's aware of how thankful Jennifer and I are for the work both of you did, but we want to say it in person." Then Scott once again turned and surveyed the room. He saw that the room and bar had been restored to its pre-wedding arrangement. The photo of him in his Braves uniform was once again on the wall behind the bar, and the photo of Dan in his Phillies uniform was in its spot just below. The arched arbor, minus the flowers, was moved over near the emergency exit.

"I see you still have the wedding arbor. Another wedding planned?" asked Scott.

"No, one of the wedding guests asked if he could rent or buy the arbor for a wedding he was planning on Tybee beach. Jaak said 'of course'—we don't expect to have any more weddings here at the Library. Jaak just asked the guy to deliver it to his home after the beach wedding. Jaak's wife Lois wants it for her flower garden."

Juri walked to the far end of the bar and waited on a customer. When he returned, he asked, "Scott, what happened to that case involving that 'Diamond Jim' guy from Atlanta?"

"It's still scheduled to go next month. Nothing new. I checked with the GBI investigator late yesterday. It's going to be a very interesting trial."

"You say *very interesting* trial? What's so special about it?"

"Any time we get a hotshot lawyer from out-of-town, it's a bit special, but this one has some added ingredients. He's the defendant along with two other defendants—his office goons. And he's the defense counsel for himself, which is rare but happens occasionally. But what makes it not only interesting but bizarre, is that he's the defense counsel for the other two."

"That's legal?"

"I don't know. I don't think the judge knows. In fact, I don't think anyone knows. I haven't heard of a case like this. If we get a conviction, I guess we'll find out on appeal. If there is an acquittal, we'll never know."

"Think you can get a conviction?"

"We wouldn't be trying him if we didn't think we could. But we have a single witness to the facts that support the crime; they have three. And I would like to cut a deal with one of the office goons, but I would have to approach him through his attorney. How do you think that would work?"

"Not too good. So, what are your chances?"

"Well, about the same as Hannibal had in marching thirty-seven elephants over the Alps on his way to Rome. And he did it. So, I have a chance."

Scott looked over at the entrance and saw Jaak coming through the door. He wasn't sure he could now find the words to fully express his thanks to both Juri and Jaak. With help from Jennifer, he did, but they both knew they had a debt that would be impossible to fully pay.

CHAPTER THIRTY
Saturday, March 28

Jessica was actually beginning to look forward to these Saturday nights at the Loca Luna Restaurant with Andy. A good meal, nice wine, and Andy was beginning to actually get the rhythm of the Latin dances she was teaching him. They found the couple they had met previously—Paul Acosta and Sheri Schauer—just arriving, and they were delighted to again share a table. Paul was the more accomplished Latin dancer, and he invited Jessica to the dance floor soon after they were seated. But Jessica was cautious not to leave Andy unattended for long, and she invited him on to the dance floor as soon as the band began one of the numbers he seemed to enjoy most. The evening seemed to pass quickly. Shortly before midnight, as both couples were leaving, Andy mentioned that he would be out of town the following weekend on an assignment related to an upcoming trial. All four agreed to meet again at the Loco Luna in two weeks—April 11.

On the way back, Andy again drove through Piedmont Park, stopping at the same spot where he had stopped the previous Saturday. It was not unexpected by Jessica. In fact, she welcomed the opportunity to once again show her commitment to "that night in Savannah" she knew Andy was anxiously awaiting. As soon as he parked, she turned to him, smiling, and began to unbutton her blouse. Andy looked on with a frozen stare but did not move. Soon she had the blouse unbuttoned and removed. She placed it on the dash in front of her. Andy remained still but wide-eyed.

In a mocking tone, Jessica said, "You are not interested. I'm hurt."

"Wrong!" Andy said, as he quickly slid over to embrace her. They kissed, and his hands began to explore just as she expected. She was aware that he was aroused, and while she welcomed it, it frightened her.

"No, no, Andy." She moved his exploring hands away. "We must wait. Not in this car; not this place. We'll be in Savannah soon. That's what I want . . . OK?"

Andy straightened up, looked into Jessica's eyes, and sighed heavily before replying. "OK . . . I guess." He then moved to the driver's side and looked pensively out the window into the partially lighted park. Then after a long moment, he turned to Jessica, smiled, and started the engine.

Once home and before getting ready for bed, she texted to Colosimo's private phone:

> "Date with Andy tonight.
> No talk about the trial.
> He seems committed to the deal.
> Still running the bases!"

She got his response the next morning.

> "Good work. I'm counting
> on you to keep him committed
> to the plan."

Chapter Thirty-One

Saturday, April 11

Andy and Jessica arrived at the Loco Luna at 7:30 p.m. They looked for their friends, Paul and Sheri, who had agreed to meet again on this date, but they had not arrived. They ordered drinks and decided to wait for their friends to arrive before ordering dinner. By 8:00 p.m., the band had set up and was playing. They danced to a few familiar songs, and when their friends had not arrived by 8:30 p.m. they ordered dinner. Paella for two. Andy asked the waiter for a good wine pairing. The waiter recommended a rosé from some obscure winery in Spain. It was reasonably priced, and Andy ordered a bottle. Both the wine and the paella proved to be good choices.

Ten o'clock, and their friends still had not arrived. That was fine with Andy, as he was anxious for a serious discussion he had been putting off.

"Jessica, I think I'm making a very big mistake if I follow the plea plan for our trial in Savannah. It's a win for Jim; Tom and I are the big losers. And I think I'm the biggest of the big losers."

Jessica was caught by surprise. She was concerned, and she knew her job was to be concerned. *Very concerned.*

"Why do you say that, Andy?"

"Because I was the least involved. True, I went with Tom to the store. But it was Jim's idea. And Tom did most of the talking. I think I could call the prosecutor and get a good deal for my testimony."

Jessica's alarm went to high alert. "But you would still have to plead. So even if you got a good deal—say probation, no jail time—you would have a conviction. So that's no solution."

"But it likely would be reduced to a misdemeanor and no jail time. Or the charges could be dismissed. The prosecutor has only one witness. He needs my testimony, and even if I came out with a misdemeanor, it beats a felony conviction. People often get admitted with a misdemeanor conviction. At least I'd have a chance at becoming a member of the bar. Tom had his chance, and he blew it years ago. If I could just pass the bar, I could get in. I had a minor offense in Alabama, but that was a long time ago. I'm sure I could pass the professional fitness part. But not with a felony conviction for witness tampering from that trial in Savannah."

"Andy, you have a good fallback career and good pay with Jim. Maybe that's your career—and you wouldn't have to take another bar. Some very intelligent law graduates fail the bar, a few fail multiple times. President Franklin Roosevelt failed the bar once, John F. Kennedy Jr. failed it twice, and Governor Pete Wilson of California failed it three times. It happens. But why go through that painful process again?"

"There's no limit on times to take it in Georgia," Andy replied. "I know I could eventually pass, just need to study, take another bar review course. I've only taken one, and there are a lot of them out there with good success rates."

"I think you are right on that, Andy. But maybe there is a better way to prepare."

"Like what?"

"Like going back to a law school—at night—and taking the courses that cover the subjects on the bar exam. You could do that beginning this summer. Free."

"Free? Where?"

"Right here in Atlanta, Adam Lansky Law School. Jim's on the board, and he says he going to ensure my admission as soon as this trial is behind us. Free. I'm sure he would do it for you, too. I could get my degree by the end of the year—I only need a half-year of courses. You already have a degree and only need some refresher courses. Jim will take care of it. Just don't let on that we are going to open up our own office next year—'McDowell and Valdez'—or maybe just 'McDowell.' How does that sound?" Jessica smiled.

Andy returned the smile. "'McDowell.' Yeah, I like that." Jessica reached for his hand, squeezed it, and continued to hold it.

The band had taken a break but was now starting up, playing "The Girl from Ipanema," the Brazillian bossa nova song that became a worldwide hit in the '60s and one of Jessica's favorites. She pulled Andy onto the dance floor and took over. She was good. Andy did the best he could, and Jessica made up for what he lacked. Before the song ended, they were the only couple left on the dance floor. Jessica was superb; Andy tried to keep up with the rhythm and occasionally was successful. At the end, they walked off to loud clapping from those who had watched. Both were smiling, excited, and exhausted.

They left the club a few minutes before midnight, and as usual, Andy took the route through Piedmont Park. He stopped his Chevy at the same spot he had stopped on their last date. The park was illuminated by the light of a half-moon and the reflected light from downtown Atlanta, only a few miles away. Jessica welcomed the stop and the familiar scene. She had been thinking about the conversation with Andy after dinner, where he expressed his fear of being the "biggest loser" if he followed the plan that would have him and Tom taking all responsibility for the alleged crime in Savannah. *He needs more encouragement from me*, she thought. The trial was fast approaching, and Jim had given her a key assignment—to make sure Andy stuck to the plan. *She would not, could not, fail.*

Tonight she would have to make that promise of a night together at the Hyatt Regency when the trial was over both vivid and enticing. She sat with her back to the passenger side door. The reflected light was sufficient for Andy to see the smile on her face. He continued to watch as she removed her blouse and placed it on the dash. Then she unhooked her bra.

"Would you like to take it the rest of the way?" she said, as the smile broadened.

Andy said, "You bet!" and quickly slid toward her, just as a large SUV pulled up and parked just a few feet away. Both Jennifer and Andy looked over at the same time. They saw the outline of two figures in the front seat. The back windows were tinted so they could not see if anyone else was in the vehicle. The two figures were not moving, but the intrusion was enough to kill the moment. Andy maintained a frozen stare at the silhouettes in the vehicle. Momentarily, a door of the SUV opened, and a light came on revealing two large men.

Andy did not wait to see if either man got out. "Damn it! We better go," he said, as he slid to the driver's side. He started his vehicle, backed out, and was quickly on his way out of the park. There were no more stops until they were at Jennifer's aunt's house and parked in the driveway. Jessica could see that there were several lights on in the house, indicating that her aunt was awake. Rather than opening her door to exit, she slid over to Andy, embraced and kissed him.

"It's OK, Andy, I'm as disappointed as you."

"Hardly; I don't think that's possible."

"We have Savannah to look forward to. Gay assured me that we are all booked at the Hyatt Regency. Tom told me that he would be driving down Saturday and you and Jim would be flying down Saturday afternoon. I'll be helping my aunt with her real estate business the entire weekend—holding open houses both Saturday and Sunday. It's part of my housing arrangements with my aunt—free bedroom and kitchen privileges for helping her on weekends. I'll drive down Sunday after work."

"Andy smiled. I didn't know you would be driving to Savannah. You'll have your Mercedes 550 with you. That's great!"

"Jim wants me to be there during jury selection. He's going to get me a copy of the jury panel name list so I can do social media research on the jurors. But that's going to be awkward and limited. I can't use my cell phone or laptop in the courtroom. I'll have to find a place close by to do the work—and I won't have much time. I hope to have at least something helpful for making challenges. He said jury selection would take most of Monday."

"I sure hope we can get a jury Monday. This waiting is getting to me."

"Andy, this trial pain will be over soon. Just stick to the plan, and the chances are good you'll be acquitted. And you have a backup deal that's a good one too. So win or lose, you and I will be celebrating at the Hyatt when it's over." She gave him another kiss. "How does that sound?"

Andy smiled. "Perfect. And I'll help you out of that blouse."

"Promise? I would like that." She leaned into him and gave him another kiss before moving back to the passenger side. She opened the door and got out. Andy walked with her to the house. They chatted briefly, kissed once again, and Andy was gone.

Jessica would have to think carefully about what new information she should text to Jim. Andy had made statements that revealed his hesitancy to follow the plan. *Have I done enough to assure his adherence?* That was her assignment; she not only welcomed it, but she had also sought it because she thought she would be good at it. And she wanted to be in the courtroom and see the disappointment on Scott Marino's face when the jury brought in the verdict of not guilty for "Diamond Jim" Colosimo. She could think of nothing else she could do to assure that verdict, and she did not want to overly concern Jim. He had enough on his mind now. So, she sent a text message to his private cell phone. It was short and simple.

> "Out with Andy tonight. No changes. He's still happy just rounding the bases with my promise of a home run at the Hyatt after the trial. (No way!).

The reply came the next morning.

"Keep him committed.
Spoke with dean at Adam
Lansky. No need to worry
about being admitted."

CHAPTER THIRTY-TWO
Monday, April 20

The trial was scheduled to start at 9:00 a.m. Scott, as usual, was there early. His boss, Felony Chief Joe Fasi, who would be serving as second chair, had not yet arrived. Jury selection was expected to take most of the day. In previous cases where Fasi and Scott had teamed up to prosecute a case, Fasi had conducted the jury selection and Scott had handled the rest of the case. However, today, Scott would conduct jury selection as well as the rest of the trial.

Scott had spent many hours thinking about the profile of the juror he wanted for this trial. When he was a student intern in the DA's office, he had been cautioned by Grady Wilder, his supervising attorney, not to put much faith in categorizing jurors by demographics or any single characteristic. Still, decisions of which juror to strike would have to be made, and that would have to be based on the information obtained from the voir dire. He recalled Wilder's advice that prosecutors were generally well served by jurors who were business owners or professionals such as accountants, insurance brokers, or dentists. Wilder had also recommended jurors who were former military officers or higher-ranking enlisted personnel. Jurors with a close connection to law enforcement personnel, such as parents or children, were a plus. Scott smiled as he recalled some additional advice from Wilder—the single exception from making juror selections based on a single characteristic: *Never accept a recent college graduate with a degree in sociology. Don't ask why; just don't do it!* So far, he had not had to reject any sociology majors.

The three defendants arrived about fifteen minutes after Scott. As expected, Colosimo was wearing his white linen suit, with diamonds adorning his hands, wrists, and necktie. Scott was sure any Chatham County jury would find him to be quite a bizarre figure, with the ostentatious diamonds, long fingernails on each little finger, and the dark rectangular mustache covering his upper lips and much of his face. His codefendants, McDowell and Reid, were in dark suits and lawyer-worthy neckties. The contrast was quite noticeable.

Richard Evans, one of the investigators for the district attorney's office, came into the courtroom and took a seat in the gallery, just behind the prosecution table. He would be available to relay messages and provide assistance as necessary. Joe Fasi arrived just a few minutes later.

Judge Feather entered the courtroom promptly at 9:00 a.m., and the bailiff walked forward with a tall wooden staff decorated with long ribbon tassels and delivered three sharp raps on the floor. This was a tradition celebrated in Georgia courts when Georgia was a British royal colony. Although abandoned in other Georgia jurisdictions, the tradition still remained in Chatham County. Scott enjoyed watching the shock of "first-timers" as the loud rapping echoed throughout the courtroom. It brought back a memory of how shocked he was the first time he heard it.

Immediately after the three raps, the bailiff roared, "All rise! The Superior Court of Chatham County, Eastern District of Georgia, is now in session, The Honorable Gail Feather, presiding." All counsel and courtroom spectators were immediately on their feet.

Judge Feather called the court to order, and the trial of James A. Colosimo, Anderson H. McDowell, and Thomas J. Reid for influencing witnesses and conspiracy to influence witnesses began.

"Before I bring in the panel of jurors for voir dire, I would like to know if either counsel has any matter I should hear first."

Scott stood. "The prosecution does not, Your Honor."

Colosimo rose slowly from the defense table to speak and of course, was careful to omit the customary words of respect, *Your Honor*. "We still have my motion for a change of venue. I previously filed a brief which included justification for moving this case out of Chatham County, and nothing has changed. Savannah is not a city where we can get a fair trial. I was the defense counsel in the Max Gordon trial last November. As I'm sure you are aware, there was a shooting on the grounds of this courthouse immediately after the verdict of not guilty, and two deaths resulted. Although I was not involved in those deaths in any way, my name as defense counsel was in the newspapers and on TV for days following. Now, less than six months later, I'm on trial as an accused in this same courthouse. The jury will connect my name with the evil acts that occurred following that November trial. That can be cured only by moving this trial to another city, away from the influence of that trial."

Scott knew this weak and specious argument would not persuade Judge Feather. He had filed a short response to the brief that Colosimo had submitted but now did not even rise to request to be heard.

Judge Feather quickly responded. "Mr. Colosimo, I am quite aware of your pending motion. A large pool of potential jurors has been summoned for this trial. If it appears that we cannot obtain a sufficient number of qualified jurors from this pool because of pre-trial publicity, I will consider moving the trial. We will begin our voir dire in a few minutes. The defense and the prosecution will have nine peremptory challenges each, so we'll need at least thirty qualified jurors from the pool in order to be sure we have a twelve-person jury. Once we have the twelve jurors to hear the case, we'll begin the selection of two alternates. Each side will have two peremptory challenges, so we will begin with a panel of at least six. Any questions?"

"I have none, Your Honor," replied Scott.

"And I have none," replied Colosimo.

"Since neither counsel has made an appearance in my court as counsel, I would like to brief you on my voir dire procedure. I will have forty members of the pool in the courtroom at once. I will ask the mandatory voir dire questions required by the Georgia Code, and I will have additional questions not required by the Code. Afterward, I will permit counsel to ask additional questions of the panel. Your voir dire questions must not cover subject areas that I have already adequately covered. You have been provided copies of the jury questionnaire form completed by each member of the panel. And yes, I realize some are incomplete and some are illegible. If you feel that something important has been omitted, then you may voir dire the juror on the missing information. Otherwise, do not ask for information that is already on a form. I expect that we will be able to complete jury selection today and begin with opening statements tomorrow morning."

Judge Feather then directed that the bailiff bring in the first forty prospective jurors. Seats had been reserved on the right side of the gallery for the overflow from the jury box. When they were seated, she briefed them on the charges and their duties.

"Each of the three defendants, James A. Colosimo, Anderson H. McDowell, and Thomas J. Reid, has been indicted on the same two charges: Count 1, influencing witnesses in violation of Section 16-10-93, Georgia Statutes, and Count 2, conspiracy to influence witnesses in violation of Section 16-4-8, Georgia Statutes. I will explain the elements of those alleged crimes at the end of the trial after all the evidence is in. It will be your duty to listen to the evidence as it is presented and then follow my instructions at the conclusion of the trial to determine whether or not any defendant is guilty of these charges." She paused briefly before continuing.

"The State is represented by Assistant District Attorney Scott Marino and Assistant District Attorney Joseph Fasi. Would you please stand." Both stood briefly and then took their seats. "The defense is represented by Mr. James Colosimo, a member of the Georgia Bar. Mr. Colosimo is a defendant named in the indictment and has chosen to represent himself at his trial. Would you stand, Mr. Colosimo." Colosimo stood briefly and took his seat.

"The other two defendants—Mr. McDowell and Mr. Reid—have also chosen to be represented by Mr. Colosimo. While you may find this unusual, an accused is entitled to counsel of his or her choice. In this case, each defendant has chosen Mr. Colosimo as counsel. You must not consider that in any way in making your decisions in this case."

The panel of jurors was sworn, and she then began voir dire, starting with the three questions required by the Georgia Code. She asked the jurors to raise a hand if any question applied to them.

"Have any of you expressed or formed an opinion in regard to the guilt or innocence of any accused?

"Do you have any prejudice or bias resting in your mind for or against any accused?"

No hands were raised after either of the first two questions. Had any of the jurors raised a hand, they would have been questioned individually at the bench.

"Is your mind perfectly impartial between the state and the accused?" was the third statutorily required question.

All raised a hand, some only after seeing all the other hands raised. She then began her additional voir dire: Did they know any of the counsel in this case? Did they know any of the accused? Know any of the witnesses? Have they read in a newspaper or heard on TV or radio anything about the case? Heard any discussion from coworkers or friends? Ever served on a jury? Been a witness? And a myriad of other questions. When there was a response from a juror, she would follow up with additional questions.

At one stage of her voir dire, she told the jurors not to raise their hand until all the questions were asked. Then she asked the following:

"Have you ever been convicted of a crime?"

"Any close member of your family ever been convicted of a crime?"

"Have any of you ever been arrested?"

"Ever been accused of a crime?"

"Ever serve on a jury in another state?"

"Ever been called for jury service in another state?"

Then she asked for a show of hands if any of the questions applied to them. If any juror raised a hand, she would call the juror to the bench for further questioning. The last two questions were put into the mix of questions because an affirmative response to any of the first four questions may be embarrassing to the juror. By adding the two additional questions, the other jurors would not know what prompted the hand raise. Scott had not observed any other judge utilizing this procedure, but he could see its value.

A question about any juror suffering "undue hardship" by serving resulted in the excusal of a Georgia State University student and a Department of Defense civilian contractor due to leave for Iraq in three days. The request of a professional musician to be excused as he needed the time to practice for an upcoming performance was denied. It was 10:45 a.m. when she turned the voir dire over to counsel, with the prosecution going first.

Scott had a list of questions he had planned to ask, but after Judge Feather completed her voir dire, none remained. This case was not like the Harrison murder trial that he had prosecuted two years previous, where there had been extensive pretrial publicity. In that case, the defendant was the son of a former senator and a candidate for Governor of Georgia—and the governor's race was ongoing and in the news daily. As a result, there was substantial interest, so much so that TV cameras were in the courtroom sending video out in real time, and about a dozen reporters attended each session of the court. This trial was nothing like that. True, there was a lot of buzz around the courthouse and among the local attorneys because of the self-representation of Colosimo and his representation of the other two defendants. The courthouse gang was debating the decision of Judge Feather to allow such representation. And while Bill Baldwin had made sure this upcoming trial was well-covered in the *South Georgia News*, it simply did not measure up to the previous sensational cases in which Scott had been involved. Judge Feather's voir dire had uncovered little interest in the case, and no one on the panel had much information about the facts. The prior case where Colosimo defended Max Gordon had been thoroughly reported in the *South Georgia News*, but apparently, it had been quickly forgotten.

Although the voir dire questions Scott had prepared had all been asked and answered, he felt he should at least ask a question or two for appearance's sake. He wanted to present an "in command" presence. He looked at one of the juror questionnaires before him and noted a juror by the name of Ralph Williams was a postal worker.

"Mr. Williams," he said, "I note that you list your occupation as a postal worker and that you have been a postal worker for nine years. Do I have that correct?"

"That is correct."

"If you are selected for this jury, you would miss several days of work. Would you be paid for the time you are away from your job?"

"Sir, I'm not sure. This is my first time being called for jury duty. I didn't ask about pay; I just told my boss I had a jury summons and would be away this week."

Scott thanked him, but he had no idea if the response helped. Scott knew if he were employed by a business or state agency, the law required that he be paid during his absence while serving on a state jury trial. But for a federal postal worker, it might be different. He already knew he had been a postal worker for nine years and had graduated from Savannah Technical College. That was good evidence of intelligence and reliability. Mr. Williams did not appear to be concerned about his pay so it was not an issue.

Scott thought that he should voir dire at least one additional juror. He leafed through the stack and selected one of the more legible forms.

"Ms. Burley, I note from your questionnaire that you served on a jury previously in a criminal case. Did anything occur in that trial that gives you concern about our criminal justice system?"

"No."

"Were you satisfied that the results were fair?"

"Yes, I was."

"What was the verdict in that trial?"

"There was a guilty verdict."

Scott was ready to turn the voir dire over to the defense. He thought he had a good feel for the "good jurors" and the "bad jurors" from the questions that Judge Feather had asked. About the only facts his questions to Mrs. Burley had produced, was that she sat on a jury that brought in a guilty verdict. He realized the facts may have demanded such a verdict, but at least he knew she could vote guilty.

He quickly conferred with his co-counsel, Fasi, who had been taking notes during the voir dire by Judge Feather.

"Ask Mr. Sullivan if he is related to Martha Sullivan," Fasi said. "She was the foreperson of the jury in the Max Gordon trial that brought in the not guilty verdict."

Scott went back to the lectern and asked the question. Mr. Sullivan replied that he was not related. Scott, still standing at the lectern, turned and looked at Fasi and received a hand motion indication he had no further questions. And with that, Scott turned the voir dire over to Colosimo.

Colosimo had much more voir dire experience than Scott and got to work quickly with numerous follow-up questions to those asked by Judge Feather. It took him only a few minutes to get back to Ms. Burley and find that she was the foreperson of her jury that brought in the guilty verdict. Scott was pretty sure she would receive a defense peremptory challenge—and regretted he had laid the groundwork for the challenge.

Colosimo's voir dire continued for almost half an hour. Judge Feather asked if Scott had any follow-up questions. He did not.

The clock in the courtroom read 11:25 a.m. The voir dire had been completed more quickly than Scott had anticipated. He had expected the voir dire to continue until at least the lunch break, and the judge would have the session for challenges and selection for alternates in the afternoon. But there were no veiled issues in the case that would need extensive voir dire. Race was not an issue—all three defendants were white, and there was no victim, except the criminal justice system.

Judge Feather turned and faced the panel of prospective jurors. "We are approaching the hour where I usually recess for lunch," she said, "but I believe we can complete jury selection this morning without going too far into the lunch hour—and you will be able to go home much earlier, with only fourteen of you having to return tomorrow. So, I'll ask the bailiff to escort you out, and we'll continue with matters for counsel only."

Just as the panel was escorted out of the courtroom so that challenges could be exercised, Scott turned to see someone approach the defense table holding some documents. The view startled him. He wondered if his eyes could be deceiving him. He sat back in his chair and gazed at the scene. No, his eyes were not deceiving him. It was indeed Jessica Valdez, and she was delivering some papers to Colosimo. The two spoke briefly, and Jessica walked to the gallery and took a seat near the front row. Scott turned to Fasi, who was busy going through the notes he had taken during the voir dire.

"Did you see that?" whispered Scott.

"See what?"

"Jessica Valdez, delivering some papers to Colosimo."

"I didn't see anyone delivering papers. Jessica Valdez? I recall the name, but can't recall much about her."

"Former office intern. I'll explain later." Scott wasn't sure what he could explain. He had no idea why she was in the courtroom or what was in the document she delivered to Colosimo. *Strange.*

There were just four challenges for cause, leaving a sufficient number on the panel to compose a twelve-person jury, even if all nine peremptory challenges available to each side were exercised. Judge Feather ordered a twenty-minute recess for counsel to discuss possible peremptory challenges. Fasi had made extensive notes and had selected just five members of the panel to challenge peremptorily. Scott agreed with the five and added another one to the list.

He wasn't sure how her voir dire responses made her unacceptable. There was just something about her that gave him concern. He recalled some additional Grady Wilder advice: when in doubt, follow your instinct. He decided he would include her in his peremptory challenges, making a total of six challenges for the prosecution.

When the twenty-minute recess was over, Judge Feather called upon counsel to make their challenges, alternating until each side had no further challenges. Scott exercised six and Colosimo eight, including the challenge—as Scott expected—against Ms. Burley.

"It appears we have sufficient qualified members from the original panel to select our two alternates," said Judge Feather. "Each side will have two strikes."

The two alternate jurors were selected. The twelve selected jury members and the two alternates were escorted into the courtroom, and the remaining members of the panel were excused. The clerk administered the oath to all fourteen jurors. They would all sit in the jury box during the trial, and the two alternates would learn they were alternates only at the end of the trial, ensuring the alternates paid as much attention to the evidence as the first twelve selected.

The jury was now in place for the trial of James A. Colosimo, Anderson H. McDowell, and Thomas J. Reid, each charged with influencing witnesses and conspiracy to influence witnesses. The trial jury consisted of seven men and five women. The alternates were both women. Judge Feather announced that the court would be in recess until 9:00 a.m. Tuesday, at which time opening statements would be presented.

Scott was pleased that the day's session was completed. He was ready to get on with the trial. He and Fasi sat at the prosecution table discussing the plans for the next day. The three defendants remained at their table also. Scott saw Jessica walking toward them. She took a seat at their table, and Scott's eyes made contact with hers. She smiled slyly, and Scott quickly turned away. He was puzzled and a bit shocked at the scene, but it was clear that Jessica was now part of the defense team. Scott and Fasi picked up their briefcases and left.

The defense team remained seated long after the prosecution team left the courtroom.

In midafternoon, Scott received a phone call from Bill Baldwin. "How's the trial looking?"

"Well, we have a jury."

"Yes, I know. I was there."

"I didn't see you. In fact, I saw few spectators."

"That's because there were few spectators to see. I was there for a short time, sitting in a back row of the gallery. Weren't but five or six others—old regulars who are there about every day. Oh, and a young lady who apparently knows you. We were seated nearby. I casually asked where she was from. She said Atlanta. So, I asked if she knew any of the counsel or the defendants. She smiled and said she knew them *all*. I guess she meant the defense counsel and his two associates. Before I could ask her any further questions, she got up with a couple of yellow pads and walked down to the defense table. I guess she had been taking notes for the defense."

"Yes, I saw her," said Scott. "You are probably right that she was there for the defense, helping evaluate the jury." He decided not to reveal that he knew her or their previous relationship—that would have just stirred up more questions from Bill, and Scott did not need that now.

"So, nothing new going on with this trial? Is that your latest report?" asked Bill with a slight chuckle.

"If there is, I'm not aware of it. I guess I'll find out in the morning."

"Good enough. See you there!"

CHAPTER THIRTY-THREE
Monday, April 20

Colosimo had informed his team—Tom, Andy, and Jessica—that he had arranged for a "celebration" Monday night at Churchill's. It was a restaurant and bar within walking distance of the Hyatt—in fact, just across the street. Colosimo always stopped there for a meal or a drink when he was in Savannah, and its location provided an added incentive for having dinner there Monday night after jury selection. It would keep his team close to the Hyatt for a good night's rest before the testimonial stage of the trial beginning the next morning. And he wanted to give them a positive report of the day's events as well as an encouraging forecast for the rest of the trial. Much of this would be for Andy's morale, to encourage him to stay with the plan.

When he made his reservations, he had requested privacy for a small party, and this being a Monday night, there was no problem with the request. The four sat at a table in an otherwise empty room. They ordered drinks, and when they arrived, Colosimo stood, held his glass out and said, "I propose a toast: 'To a successful trial—and bonuses for all!'" They all laughed, repeated the toast, and clicked their glasses against Colosimo's.

"We're off to a good start. We have a superb jury. Several mistakes by the prosecution in their strikes, and thanks to Jessica and her social media expertise, we avoided a few. Excellent research work this morning, Jessica. Especially for finding that lady with her three grandsons in Atlanta—two cops and a prosecutor. Do you recall her name?"

"Evelyn Hinesly," said Jessica. "She was really proud of all the criminals they had helped put away. About one a day, according to her Facebook postings."

"She hadn't mentioned that during her voir dire. Probably anxious to get on a criminal jury to do her share. But sayonara, Evelyn. Jessica also discovered a good one for us. That juror's Facebook gripe was the prosecution of her nephew. Do you recall her name, Jessica?"

"Judy Hastings. She never posted where her nephew was tried—could have been here in Savannah. And she didn't say what the charges were—only that it was such a travesty of justice. Good guy caught up in a bad justice system. She is really bitter. I think she'll carry it into the jury room."

"None of that came out in the voir dire. Just a nice lady willing to serve is what I got from her answers. Prosecutors must have gotten the same feeling. She was very outspoken in her answers. Could become the foreperson. We can hope. But anyway, I'm satisfied with our jury. I'm confident we'll have an outcome to celebrate when we get back to Atlanta."

Jessica caught Andy's eye and privately gave him a wink and a smile. She hoped he would understand she was underscoring the celebration she had promised. He smiled back.

The conversation then turned to sports, travel, TV, and movies. Dinner was ordered and served, and as the evening was drawing to a close, Colosimo looked at Jessica and said, "We need to discuss your assignment for tomorrow." Then, looking at Reid, he said, "Tom, use the firm credit card and settle up here. I'll walk back with Jessica so we can talk." And with that, he stood. "I've enjoyed the evening immensely and look forward to tomorrow." Jessica was now standing. Together, she and Colosimo walked out of the restaurant and crossed the street to the Hyatt Regency.

When they entered the lobby, Colosimo stopped and turned to Jessica. "This will be a short trial. Not many witnesses, but I doubt we can finish in one day. I think the prosecution may be finished by midafternoon. So, if I can start our case, I'll put Tom on first and Andy second. I'm sure we won't get to closing. But I would like to get Andy on tomorrow, and you know why. I don't want him to have another night to consider any options. The risk of his breaking the pact gets more critical as he gets more stressed. So, Jessica, if he doesn't testify tomorrow, I want you to spend some time with him tomorrow night. Take him to your favorite restaurant. Just the two of you. Promise him *anything* if you think he's wavering. *Anything.* He appears strong now, but I've had enough clients panic in the courtroom to know things can change quickly. I'm counting on you. By the way, have you heard from Adam Lansky Law School? I asked them to expedite your admission."

"Not yet; hopefully it will be waiting for me when we get back to Atlanta."

Colosimo walked to the bar for a nightcap. Jessica went to her room and prepared for bed. One more night out with Andy was not something to bring good dreams, but at least this charade was ending, and she would soon be back in law school.

CHAPTER THIRTY-FOUR

Tuesday, April 21

It was shortly after 9:00 a.m. when Judge Feather looked toward the two men seated at the prosecution table. "The prosecution may make its opening statement."

Scott rose with some papers in his hand, quickly walked forward and placed the papers on the lectern in the center of the courtroom. The papers were an outline of his opening statement. He did not expect to need them, but they were there just in case. He then walked toward the jury and stood about twelve feet in front of the first row.

"May it please the court and members of the jury," he began. "On Monday, October 5 of last year, two men visited a small convenience store located at 1443 Waters Avenue, here in Savannah. It was late at night, and the only person on duty at the store was the owner. But these two men were not there to purchase cigarettes or groceries. They were there for an entirely different purpose. That purpose was to influence the owner not to testify as a witness in a trial here in Savannah involving the crime of perjury. The name of that store owner was Vijay Patel."

Scott walked over and stood by the defense table before proceeding. "And the two men who entered the store with the purpose of influencing Mr. Patel not to testify, are seated at this table. They are Anderson H. McDowell and Thomas J. Reid." Scott pointed to each defendant as he gave their names. He then returned to his position in front of the jury.

"It was on that date that the crime of influencing witnesses was committed in Savannah, but the conspiracy—the plan—for this visit was made in the days prior to that, in Atlanta, Georgia. You see, members of the jury, Mr. McDowell and Mr. Reid were employees of an Atlanta law firm that was defending the perjury trial, and Vijay Patel was a vital witness for the prosecution. The owner of this law firm planned and conspired with those two men—his employees—to make that visit to Savannah for the purpose of influencing Mr. Patel not to testify." Scott walked over to near the defense table before continuing.

"And the owner of that law firm, the only licensed attorney in the firm, was this defendant, James E. Colosimo." Scott pointed directly at Colosimo for a long moment after he called his name. Colosimo folded his arms across his chest confidently and looked at the jury with a broad smile. Scott then returned to his position in front of the jury.

"You will learn that the visit that night to this small convenience store accomplished exactly what the conspirators had hoped to accomplish. Mr. Patel, one of the prosecution's primary witnesses for the perjury trial, was influenced not to testify. In fact, on the day he was to testify at the perjury trial, he was confronted by one of the two men when he arrived at the courthouse. This resulted in his departure from the courthouse and from Savannah. He spent the rest of that day at Tybee Island. So, members of the jury, the trial today is for two crimes committed by each of these three defendants: First, influencing witnesses, and second, conspiring to influence witnesses. At the end of this trial, after all the evidence is in, Judge Feather will explain that these are separate and individual crimes under Georgia statutes.

"This will not be a long trial, and it will not be a difficult case. We will prove the charges with just four witnesses. First, you will hear from Carl DeBickero, an agent with the Georgia Bureau of Investigation. He will tell you about his investigation and the arrest of Mr. Reid and Mr. McDowell and how his investigation led to the grand jury indictment of these two defendants, as well as their boss, Mr. Colosimo. He will tell you that when Mr. Reid was questioned as to why he was at the convenience store on that Monday, he replied he was in Savannah to interview witnesses and do whatever is necessary to get the case ready for trial for his boss.

"You will hear from Luke Schaub, the defense counsel who was representing Mr. Patel at the time. He will tell you that he had sternly cautioned Mr. Patel not to discuss his case with anyone. You will also hear the testimony of the deputy who picked up Mr. Patel at Tybee Island, the day after he failed to appear at trial to testify.

"And you will also hear the testimony of Mr. Patel. Let me tell you a bit about Mr. Patel. He has lived in Savannah since his discharge from the United States Coast Guard. He is a family man who owns and operates a small convenience store on Waters Avenue here in Savannah. I won't present him to you as a saint—he is not—but he had lived his life with no criminal involvement until he received an offer of substantial money to testify falsely in a trial in this very courthouse. I suppose it offers some proof of the old saying that 'everyone has a price.' In this case, a quarter of a million dollars. Apparently, that met Mr. Patel's price, as Mr. Patel accepted the money, and he did, in fact, testify falsely. He will admit it to you. And he has paid a price and will continue to pay a price for his crime. He was charged with the crime of perjury and conspiracy to commit perjury, along with the other persons involved in the crime. One of the other persons who was charged was a Chicago attorney by the name of Max Gordon. He was the attorney who was defending the perjury charge.

"Perhaps you wonder about the source of such a large sum of money that was offered to Mr. Patel, and I can understand your curiosity. But it's not relevant to the case you will be hearing today. What is relevant is that Mr. Patel accepted a pretrial agreement to plead guilty and testify for the prosecution in its case against attorney Max Gordon. In exchange for his truthful testimony, he would receive a more lenient sentence, but one which included 12 months confinement. His trial was scheduled for a date after the Max Gordon trial.

"Although Mr. Patel had a pretrial agreement that limited his sentence, he was stressed and frightened of his future and greatly concerned about the embarrassment and financial damage he had brought upon his family. When Mr. McDowell and Mr. Reid entered his convenience store that night, this stress had been on his mind constantly since his arrest four months previous. He was in a desperate situation. So, when he was visited late that night at his store by Mr. Reid and Mr. McDowell, he was an easy mark for their influence.

"Business was slow, and he had let his cashier off early. Defendant Reid told Mr. Patel that he had information—free information that would show him a way out of his criminal trial. Mr. Patel told the defendants that he had been instructed by his counsel not to discuss his case with anyone. The two men told him he did not have to discuss it with them, all he would have to do is just listen to them. They assured him that there was an easy way out of the charges against him, that the prosecution couldn't prove that he lied. That it takes two witnesses to prove the charge, and there were not two witnesses against him. They told Mr. Patel that his defense counsel was just offering him up on a platter to the prosecution. They suggested that perhaps Mr. Patel's attorney had not told him of this sure defense because he needed a favor from the prosecution in another case or perhaps money had exchanged hands. The visit left him very concerned about the advice he was getting from his defense counsel, but he was afraid to even mention his concern to his defense counsel—or the visit by the two men—because his attorney had given him strict advice not to discuss the case with anyone. He was very confused but still planned to testify.

"On the day he was scheduled to testify, he went to the courthouse for that purpose. Standing near the entrance was one of the men who had visited him and informed him of how he could beat the charge. He stopped momentarily, and the man looked at him and said something that made him reconsider his plan to testify. He left the courthouse and drove to Tybee where he was picked up by a sheriff's deputy the next morning. Thus, the Max Gordon jury never heard the evidence that could be presented by the key witness, Vijay Patel.

"Members of the jury, that is briefly the evidence we will present. And when we complete the presentation of all the evidence, I am confident you will return a verdict that speaks the truth, that all three defendants are guilty of each of the two charges beyond all reasonable doubt. Thank you." Scott returned to the prosecution table.

Judge Feather looked at the defense table and asked, "Mr. Colosimo, would you like to make your opening statement now, or reserve it?"

"We wish to make an opening statement now and also just before we begin presenting our evidence," responded Colosimo.

"You may make only one opening statement," responded Judge Feather. "You may make it now, or reserve it and make it later before you begin your case in chief."

"I am defending two accused, plus myself. I should be entitled to make at least two opening statements."

Judge Feather called the attorneys to the bench for a conference out of the hearing of the jury. Once they were standing before her, she quietly said, "Yes, Mr. Colosimo, you are defending two codefendants plus yourself. And I tried very hard to dissuade you from that. However, you and your codefendants firmly stated that your defenses were one and the same. That being the case, you will be permitted one and only one opening statement. Do you wish to make it now, or reserve it?"

"This is a very serious violation of my due process rights and my two clients' due process rights. I object and want my objection stated strongly on the record."

"I'm sure you are aware that this sidebar is being recorded and will be part of the record. I'm not sure how the reporter will be able to place it 'strongly' on the record, but it will be there. Now, do you wish to make your one and only opening statement now, or reserve it?"

"We'll reserve it."

"Very well. Counsel may return to your seats." There was a smile on Scott's face as he returned to the prosecution table with Fasi.

When counsel were all seated, Judge Feather turned to the jury. "Counsel for the defense has chosen to reserve his opening statement. That means he will be able to make his opening statement after the prosecution rests. The prosecution may now call its first witness."

CHAPTER THIRTY-FIVE

Tuesday, April 21

Scott rose and announced, "The State calls Carl DeBickero."

DeBickero was sworn and was asked a number of introductory questions which revealed his employment with the Georgia Bureau of Investigation and his assignment to the case. Scott and DeBickero had gone over his testimony carefully to make sure there was no slip up by DeBickero in testifying about his arresting Reid and McDowell for another crime which occurred three months before the Max Gordon trial. The two had driven to Savannah with a prostitute who made a false accusation against Scott. The expectation was that such an accusation would result in Scott's removal as the prosecutor in the Max Gordon case, which Colosimo was defending. The scheme was unraveled by DeBickero, and he arrested both Reid and McDowell. Shortly after their arrests for that criminal act, DeBickero also arrested the two for influencing witnesses, the charges in this case. Scott asked the District Attorney not to proceed with the false accusation charge. He did not want his name to come up in the prosecution of such a sordid case, and, of course, he would have been prohibited from serving as prosecutor. The influencing witnesses charge was more serious, and he wanted to be the prosecutor assigned. The District Attorney agreed. So now, he and DeBickero had to be careful not to refer to that first arrest or crime, as it would likely result in a mistrial.

"Agent DeBickero, when were you first assigned to this case?"

"I was assigned to the case on November 19, 2008. That was the day after Mr. Patel failed to comply with his subpoena to testify in the Max Gordon trial."

"What events led to your assignment?"

"I was the agent assigned to the Max Gordon case and was at the courthouse during the trial. I was aware that Mr. Patel had failed to appear to testify for the prosecution. After the closing arguments had been heard, the trial judge ordered a short recess just before he was to give instructions to the jury. During that time, I was in the courtroom speaking with the prosecutors when Attorney Luke Schaub came in with the news that Mr. Patel had been located and was being detained at the county detention center. Attorney Schaub was Mr. Patel's defense attorney. Patel's failure to appear and testify dealt a severe blow to the prosecution's case against Max Gordon, and because I was the agent on the Gordon trial, I expected I would be assigned to investigate any case against Mr. Patel. My office is in Statesboro, about an hour's drive from Savannah. And because I was already in Savannah, I thought I should get on it right away. So, I placed a call to my boss in Statesboro. He agreed, so that's what led to my assignment."

"How did you proceed with your investigation?" asked Scott.

"Attorney Schaub informed me of some of the information he received from the officer who brought Patel to the detention center. Apparently, Patel had given the officer his reasons for skipping the trial. I wanted to interview Mr. Patel immediately. Since I knew he was already represented by an attorney—Mr. Schaub—I asked Mr. Schaub if he could meet me at the detention center so that I could interview Mr. Patel. Mr. Schaub said he would speak with Mr. Patel first so he could advise him. He said he would let me know if his client agreed to speak with me and that he would meet me at the detention center."

"Did you interview Mr. Patel?"

"Yes, with Mr. Schaub present."

"What were the results of that interview?"

"Mr. Patel explained why he failed to appear to testify and provided the names of two men who were involved in his failure to appear. I obtained a sworn statement from Mr. Patel and later arrested the two men here in Savannah. They were Thomas Reid and Anderson McDowell."

"Were you familiar with the two men before their arrest?"

"I knew they worked for Mr. Colosimo's law firm."

"Do you see Mr. Colosimo in the courtroom?"

"Yes. He's the man seated in the middle at the defense table." DeBickero pointed.

"If you see the two men you arrested—Mr. Reid or Mr. McDowell— in court today, please point to them, stating each name."

"Yes, that's Mr. Reid on the right of Mr. Colosimo," he said, pointing. "Mr. McDowell is on his left."

"After arresting these two men, did you interview them?"

"Yes, and at the time, I advised them of their Miranda rights. I interviewed each, separate from the other."

Scott asked DeBickero to explain exactly how he advised them. DeBickero explained in detail, using a Miranda warning card he had on him. He explained they both said they understood their rights and agreed to answer his questions.

"I asked them why they were in Savannah on Monday, October 5, 2008. Reid replied that they were there to interview witnesses and otherwise prepare for a case their law firm would be defending the following month. I asked if they had visited Mr. Patel at his convenience store. Reid admitted they had—he could hardly deny it, knowing that most convenience stores have security cameras working twenty-four-seven. I asked why they had paid the visit so late at night. Reid replied, 'As I said, I interview witnesses and take statements and do whatever is necessary to get the case ready for trial for my boss.' I then asked if they obtained a statement from Mr. Patel, and neither responded. I waited. After a long moment, Mr. Reid said they did not wish to answer any further questions and the interview ended."

"What further action did you take on the case?"

"I prepared my report including the sworn statement of Mr. Patel and forwarded it to the District Attorney. Later I testified before the grand jury, which resulted in the indictments against the three defendants in this case."

"I have no further questions."

"Do you wish to cross-examine, Mr. Colosimo?" asked Judge Feather.

"Of course." Colosimo rose and walked slowly to the lectern. The broad array of diamonds on his person and clothing glistened in the brightly lit courtroom.

"Mr. DiPickaro . . ." Before he could go further, he was interrupted by the witness.

"It's DeBickero, Sir."

"Oh, touchy, I see."

"No, just prefer accuracy. And it makes it easier for the court reporter."

"Well, Mr. DEE Bickero, you told the jury that you have been employed as a GBI agent for fourteen years, is that correct?"

"Yes."

"During those fourteen years, have you found that many witnesses get their facts wrong, even when trying to tell the truth?"

"Yes."

"And many get their facts wrong because they are lying?"

"Correct."

"In this case, Mr. Patel was not only a witness, but he was facing the same charges as Mr. Gordon, correct?"

"That's essentially correct, except Mr. Patel was testifying under a pretrial agreement that would have dismissed one of his charges had he testified."

"You mean testified as the prosecutor wanted him to testify, don't you?"

"No, I mean testify and testify truthfully."

"Whether he testified truthfully would be determined by the prosecutor, correct?"

"To obtain his pretrial agreement, he submitted a statement with the help of his defense counsel. This statement was consistent with the facts that I had uncovered during my investigation that resulted in the Gordon trial. His testimony would be considered 'truthful' if it was consistent with the facts learned from that investigation."

"You just don't want to answer the question, do you, Mr. DEE Bickero? I asked if it was the prosecutor who would determine if he testified truthfully. Just answer the question."

"Yes, of course, initially the prosecutor would determine if the witness had testified truthfully."

"Those 'facts' that you say were uncovered during your investigation were mostly provided by Mr. Patel, correct?"

"Yes."

"And during all your conversations with Mr. Patel, he did not mention my name, did he?"

"No."

"So, you have no information that directly connects me to influencing witnesses as charged in the indictment, do you?"

"I believe I do. Mr. Reid and Mr. McDowell are your employees. You direct their work, and Mr. Reid claimed they had visited Mr. Patel 'to get the case ready for trial for their boss.' Even without that statement, these two employees of yours would not have driven to Savannah for a Monday night visit to Mr. Patel without your knowledge and consent."

"I did not ask you to make the closing argument for the prosecution. I asked if you had any information directly connecting me to influencing witnesses as charged. And the answer to that appears to be 'no.'" Colosimo turned from the witness, saying, "I have no further questions."

Scott rose and looked at Judge Feather. "Your Honor, I object to counsel misinterpreting the witness's answer as 'no.' That is not what the witness said. I request it be stricken."

"The jury has heard the testimony. They are the ones who will interpret the response of the witness. Do you wish to redirect?"

Scott thought that DeBickero had done well with his testimony. As Colosimo had said, he had made "the closing" for the prosecution. What else could DeBickero add? He would just call his next witness.

"No, Your Honor. No redirect."

"Then I think we'll take a short recess." Judge Feather looked at the courtroom clock. "The court will be in recess until 10:30."

Scott stood, and for the first time, gazed around the courtroom. The gallery seemed to be filled to capacity, and now everyone seemed to be moving, either coming or going. He did note Bill Baldwin in his usual front row seat, busy writing on a note pad. He noted someone else, just two seats away from Bill. It was Jessica. Standing beside her was one of the defendants, Anderson McDowell. They were engaged in a conversation, and both were smiling. Scott took his seat again, had a short conversation with Fasi, and began reviewing his notes.

Soon Judge Feather entered and called the court to order, and Scott called his next witness, Luke Schaub. Schaub was sworn, and Scott asked him a few questions to introduce him to the jury and establish that he was an attorney practicing criminal law in Savannah.

"Mr. Schaub, do you know a man by the name of Vijay Patel?"

"Yes, he is a client of mine."

"Were you representing him on October 5, 2008—last year?"

"Yes."

"What were the charges?"

"He was charged with accepting $250,000 to testify falsely in a trial. The indictment was for perjury and conspiracy to commit perjury."

"Was anyone else charged in those crimes?"

"Yes, a Chicago attorney by the name of Max Gordon. Gordon was the defense counsel at the trial where Mr. Patel was charged with committing the perjury. Gordon was charged with subordination of perjury."

"What is 'subordination of perjury?'"

"'Subordination of perjury' is the crime of persuading a person to commit perjury."

"On October 5, 2008, what was the status of the Gordon case?"

"It was scheduled for trial, to begin Monday, November 17, 2008."

"On October 5, 2008, what was the status of the case against Mr. Patel?"

"His trial was pending. I had worked out a pretrial agreement with the prosecutor. For Mr. Patel's truthful testimony against Max Gordon, his maximum punishment would be no more than one-year confinement. His trial would not be held until after the Gordon trial, giving him the opportunity to testify in the Gordon case according to the pretrial agreement."

"Had you discussed with Mr. Patel any potential defenses to the charges?"

"Yes, based on my investigation of the charges and the facts provided by Mr. Patel, we discussed various strategies and defenses. But the State had a strong case. We were very unlikely to win, and when the state offered a favorable pretrial agreement, on my advice Mr. Patel accepted the agreement."

"In considering the defenses, did you consider a defense based on the 'two-witness rule'?"

"Yes, I considered that rule, which applies to the crime of perjury. Proving perjury requires two witnesses or only one witness with corroborating circumstances. The State had ample corroborating circumstances, and it would have been a losing strategy."

"Had you given Mr. Patel any instructions concerning his discussing his case with others?"

"Yes. I had given him specific instructions on more than one occasion to not discuss his case with anyone but me. And I told him if anyone attempted to discuss the case with him, to notify me immediately."

"Thank you. I have no further questions."

"Cross-examination, Mr. Colosimo?" asked Judge Feather.

"Yes, I will." Colosimo stood and walked to the lectern. "Mr. Schaub, other than what your client told you, you have no evidence as to why he did not testify, do you?"

"No, I do not"

"Mr. Patel did not mention my name to you, correct?"

"Correct."

"The truth is, you have no personal knowledge of any facts connecting me to this alleged crime, isn't that correct?"

"Yes."

"I have no further questions."

"Redirect, Mr. Marino?"

"No, Your Honor."

"Then call your next witness."

"The State calls Edward Jettinghoff," announced Scott.

Jettinghoff was the deputy who picked up Patel on Tybee Island the morning after he failed to appear for trial. He had a very revealing conversation with Patel during their ride to the detention center. Patel told the deputy of the late-night visit by Reid and McDowell to his store in October. Patel also explained to the deputy that he had in fact gone to the courthouse to testify but left after being confronted by one of the two men who had visited him at his store. Scott would have welcomed this testimony from the deputy as it would have shown consistency in Patel's story. But all of it was inadmissible as it was hearsay, and it would not even be offered. About all Jettinghoff could offer was that he found Patel out on Tybee Island, detained him, and drove him to the detention center. He merely filled in the timeline from Patel's failure to appear at trial to his interview by GBI agent DeBickero. It also gave a bit of credence to Patel's claim that he departed the courthouse after being confronted by one of the men who had visited him that Monday night.

However, Scott had another reason for calling Jettinghoff as a witness. Grady Wilder, Scott's former mentor, had advised Scott that the more witnesses, the better the chances for a conviction, even if some of the witnesses had little—or nothing—to add to the evidence. These would often be first responders or extra members of a forensic team. According to Wilder, presenting only one or two witnesses leaves the jurors thinking *this is a weak case if this is all you have*. Jettinghoff had little to add other than being a link to Patel being in custody—sort of a "first responder."

Colosimo had no cross-examination. The witness had not hurt his case and cross-examination would run the chance of creating an opening for the hearsay to come in.

Judge Feather called counsel to the bench for a conference. "How many more witnesses do you have, Mr. Marino?"

"One, Your Honor. Mr. Patel. His testimony will be a bit longer than the other witnesses."

"It is somewhat earlier than I usually take lunch recess, but if we take it now, we can reconvene promptly at 1:00. We'll hear your final witness, followed by Mr. Colosimo's opening and then his witnesses, if any."

"We haven't yet determined if we will have any witnesses," said Colosimo. Scott knew this was a lie. Perhaps Colosimo would not take the stand, but his two codefendants—the Monday night visitors to Patel's convenience store—would surely testify. He wasn't even asked if he would have any witnesses. Just a gratuitous lie, par for his team.

Judge Feather informed the jury they would be taking an early lunch break and would reconvene at 1:00 p.m., adding the usual cautionary instruction of not discussing the case during the break.

CHAPTER THIRTY-SIX
Tuesday, April 21

"The State calls Vijay Patel," announced Scott shortly after the court reconvened at 1:00 p.m., his voice giving notice that this was an important witness. Patel was a veteran witness. He had testified in the two previous Harrison trials that Scott had helped prosecute. Nevertheless, he appeared frightened and shaky. This despite the fact that Scott had gone over his expected testimony several times, and his attorney, Luke Schaub, who had testified earlier, was at the courthouse giving him moral support.

Scott started the questioning of his star witness with the usual "name, address, and occupation," but he needed more to establish his credibility which was sure to later come under a blistering attack from Colosimo. His background: born and raised in Los Angeles, served in the United States Coast Guard, stationed for three years at Tybee Island, met his wife while stationed there, was honorably discharged, and settled in Savannah, where he had managed a small convenience store on Waters Avenue for the past twenty years. He had expected Colosimo to object to some of these questions as "bolstering" or "irrelevant," but Colosimo had remained quiet. Scott thought of going further with background questions, such as number of children, their ages, occupations, etc., but decided to stop while ahead.

"Mr. Patel, do you recall where you were on the night of October 5, 2008?"

"Yes, I was at my store, Fast Eddies, at 1443 Waters Avenue, here in Savannah."

"What type of store is Fast Eddies?"

"It's a small convenience store in a mostly residential neighborhood."

"Was this a busy night at your store?"

"No, it was a Monday and a slow night. I had let my cashier off early. I was minding the store alone."

"Now directing your attention to about 10:30 that night, did anything unusual occur?"

"Yes, two men came in who wanted to discuss my upcoming trial."

"Do you see those two men in the courtroom?"

"Yes."

"Would you please point to them."

Patel pointed at the defense table. "They are the two men on each side of the man in the middle with the big black mustache."

"Do you know their names?"

"I do now, but not that night. They are Thomas Reid and Anderson McDowell. The one on the left of the guy in the middle is McDowell."

"You say you were facing an upcoming trial?"

"Yes."

"What were the charges against you, Mr. Patel?"

"I was charged with perjury. I was offered $250,000 to testify falsely. I took the money and did it."

"You admit you testified falsely?"

"Yes."

"Have you had your trial on that charge?"

"Yes, just recently. I pleaded guilty. I had a pretrial agreement that my attorney worked out with the prosecutor. But at the time of the visit that night by those two men, I had not gone to trial, but I had a pretrial agreement for my testimony if I did testify."

"Mr. Patel, are you testifying today under the terms of a pretrial agreement?"

"Yes."

"What are the terms of the agreement?"

"For my truthful testimony, the prosecutor has agreed to ask the judge to limit my sentence to no more than twelve months confinement plus a fine of five hundred dollars."

Scott chose to bring this out during his case in chief. It would definitely come out eventually. And while it certainly was not something that brought credit to a witness, Scott thought it preferable to bring it out now rather than giving the defense an "a-ha!" moment on cross-examination.

"Were those who offered you the $250,000 also charged?"

"Yes."

"Do you know their names?"

"One was a lawyer by the name of Max Gordon. He was charged."

"And his trial—was that the one where you failed to appear?"

"Yes. When those two men," responded Patel, pointing directly at McDowell and Reid, "came to visit me at my store, I had already been offered a pretrial agreement by the prosecution to be a witness against Gordon. I had accepted the pretrial agreement and was awaiting the trial. The trial was about a month away."

"What was your mental and emotional condition at the time, Mr. Patel?"

"Objection!" Colosimo was on his feet, his right hand shaking violently as if it were on fire. Scott was startled by the sudden awakening of the defense counsel. Before the trial began, he had expected Colosimo to be in a perpetual objection mode, but this was his first objection of the trial.

Colosimo continued with his objection. "Only an expert—a psychiatrist or psychologist—is qualified to answer that question and this witness is neither."

Scott had anticipated that there would be an objection to this question on "relevancy" grounds and had prepared a response to such an objection. And before he could think of a response to this different objection, Judge Feather quietly responded, "Overruled."

Scott could not suppress a smile as the diamond decorated defense counsel sat and quickly—and with emphasis—folded his arms across his chest.

"You may answer the question, Mr. Patel."

"I was very afraid of what was coming. Who would look out for my family while I was in jail? I was embarrassed at what I had done. I was so ashamed. I couldn't sleep, I was just hopeless, really down."

"What did these men tell you, Mr. Patel?"

"They could help me. They said they knew a way out of the charge against me. That the prosecutor could not prove it."

"Did they give you any reason for the prosecutor not being able to prove the charge?"

"They said the 'two-witness' rule was the reason. I had never heard of that. They said two witnesses would be required to prove it, and the prosecutor didn't have two witnesses. They told me the pretrial agreement worked out by my attorney was just a way of serving me up on a platter to the prosecutor."

"Did they offer any reason why your defense counsel would do that?"

"Yes. They said that maybe my defense counsel did not know what was required to prove the charge, or perhaps he was working with the prosecutor. They said maybe money had changed hands or maybe my defense counsel needed a favor from the prosecutor for somebody else he was defending."

"Did they tell you why they were telling you this?"

"Well, not exactly. They just said they stood for justice. That's the only reason they gave. They didn't tell me that they worked for the attorney who was defending the case. I didn't ask them any questions, I just listened. My attorney had instructed me not to discuss the case with anyone, so I didn't ask questions. I just listened to what they were saying."

"What, if anything, did they tell you to do?"

"They told me to follow a three-part plan. First, not to be a 'sacrificial lamb.' That was the term they used. I knew that was to plead not guilty, to abandon the pretrial agreement I had signed. Second, to look up the two-witness rule on the Internet and compare it with what they had been telling me. And third, consider very carefully whether to discuss what they told me with my attorney and to ask myself whether I could trust him to give me a truthful answer."

"What did you do after the two men left your store?"

"I had a computer in my office, so I locked up, turned off the lights, and went to my computer. I entered 'two-witness rule.' I got a lot of links to different things—bible references and the U.S. Constitution regarding treason. Then I found a link that said it was a rule in some states that required two witnesses to prove perjury. But it didn't say what states required it. I didn't know how to find out if Georgia was one of those states, but I knew the librarians at the Bull Street library would help me. My oldest daughter had gone there for help with some of her school work, and she spoke highly of them."

"Did you go there for help?"

"I was there when they opened up the next morning. I just asked if there was someone in the reference department who could find out if the two-witness rule for perjury was the rule in Georgia. This lady I talked to said she wasn't an attorney, but she could look up what the Georgia statute says. She got to work on her computer and told me yes, in Georgia the statute reads that a single witness was not sufficient, but corroborating circumstances may serve as the second witness. I asked her what that meant, and she said I should see a lawyer for that advice. So, I was confused. And I was afraid to bring this up with my attorney because he had told me in no uncertain terms that I was not to discuss my case with anyone but him."

"So, what did you decide to do about your confusion?"

"I decided to just stick with my attorney. I was stressed and losing sleep, but I didn't see another alternative. I was afraid to tell my attorney about the visit from the two men."

"So, you planned to testify?"

"Yes."

"What changed your mind?"

"When I got to the courthouse, just inside the entryway, I saw one of the men who had visited me that night. I didn't know his name then, but I do now."

"What is his name?"

"Anderson McDowell."

"What happened when you saw Mr. McDowell?"

"He just looked at me and said, 'Are you stupid?' That was all he said. But it made me think again about my options. I was tired, stressed—and had not slept but a few hours in the past three or four days. So, I turned around, got in my car, and drove out to Tybee. Just walked up and down the beach. Spent the night in my car. Next morning, I got up and started wandering again. I guess someone got suspicious of my wandering around in a suit—I was still dressed for court. An officer stopped me and asked my name. Before long, a deputy from the sheriff's department came and took me to the detention center."

"Looking back on your failure to testify that day, tell this jury in your own words, what caused you to fail to testify at that trial."

"It was that visit by Mr. Reid and McDowell and the things they said that night."

"I have no further questions," said Scott.

Judge Feather looked at the defense table and said, "You may cross-examine, Mr. Colosimo."

Colosimo stood and adjusted his diamond-studded necktie. In accomplishing that task, he first extended his hands and wrists from his coat sleeves, revealing his diamond-studded watch and his diamond-studded fingers. Seemingly pleased with his appearance of affluence, he then moved his hands to the sides of his head and smoothed his heavily gelled hair. Now apparently satisfied with this total visual impact, he continued to the lectern. He had no visible notes when he began his cross-examination.

"Mr. Patel, I listened closely to your testimony. I did not hear you mention that these two men threatened to injure you. And that's because they did not threaten to injure you, correct?"

"Correct, they did not threaten to injure me."

"And they did not threaten to damage any property of yours, did they?"

"No, they did not."

"And they did not threaten to injure any member of your family, did they?"

"No."

"In fact, they did not threaten you in any manner whatsoever, did they?"

"No."

"And they did not make any promise to reward you with money for not testifying, did they?"

"No."

"In fact, Mr. Patel, they did not offer you any reward, benefit, or consideration in any form or manner whatsoever, did they?"

"No."

"Mr. Patel, are you aware that I have been charged in this case with the same charges that Mr. Reid and McDowell are charged?"

"Yes, I am."

"Did these men mention my name to you?"

"No."

"Did you hear my name at any time during your conversation with these two men?"

"No."

"I have no further questions of the witness."

Colosimo turned from the lectern and took to his seat at the defense table.

Scott rose and faced Judge Feather. "No redirect, Your Honor, and the prosecution rests."

Judge Feather looked at the courtroom clock. "We will take a twenty-minute recess now," she said. "Bailiff, please escort the jury to the jury room."

Judge Feather called the court to order with the jury absent. She anticipated a motion by the defense, which must be heard out of the presence of the jury.

And as she expected, Colosimo was on his feet immediately. "The defense moves for a judgment of acquittal of all charges against Mr. Reid and Mr. McDowell. The charges have not been proved beyond all reasonable doubt. There has been no evidence of threats, intimidation, physical force, or promises of benefits. The only thing the prosecution has proved is that Mr. Reid and Mr. McDowell informed Mr. Patel of his rights. That is no crime. That should be welcomed by Mr. Patel and applauded by everyone interested in a fair trial. Justice demands that this motion be granted. And I make the same motion for myself. For the charges against me, there is no evidence whatsoever—none—to connect me to these alleged crimes. Charging me was a travesty from the start—proving the grand jury was under the complete control of the District Attorney. This motion must be granted as to each defendant."

"Do you wish to be heard, Mr. Marino?"

"I do, Your Honor. These three defendants were indicted under Section 16-10-93, Georgia Statutes. Under the statute, it is the crime of 'Influencing Witnesses' to engage in misleading conduct toward another with intent to influence or prevent the testimony of any person in an official proceeding. Neither threats, intimidation, physical force, or promises of benefits are a requirement, although these acts would also be violations of the statute. It is clear from the evidence that Mr. Reid and Mr. McDowell—both employees of Mr. Colosimo—traveled to Savannah with the intent to ensure that Mr. Patel did not testify in the Max Gordon case and that they confronted Mr. Patel with false or misleading statements to carry out that intent. It was clearly a conspiracy, and they were successful. To suggest that Mr. Colosimo was not part of the plan is surely beyond the imagination of anyone who listened to the evidence. It is inconceivable that these two employees drove to Savannah and acted alone without his input. Mr. Reid stated they were in Savannah to get the case ready for trial. And that they did—they convinced the key witness in the case to skip the trial. Taken in the light most favorable to the prosecution—which is the legal test for this motion—the prosecution has proved both crimes against each defendant beyond any reasonable doubt."

Judge Feather waited a long moment before speaking. "The motion is denied as to each defendant. Mr. Colosimo, you will have the opportunity to make an opening statement before presenting your case. We will take a short recess now and reconvene at 3:00."

CHAPTER THIRTY-SEVEN
Tuesday, April 21

During the recess, Colosimo and his two associates remained at the defense table for a last-minute strategy session. Nothing really had occurred during the trial that was unexpected.

"I think the case is going fairly well for our defense," he quietly assured his two associates. "They have proved nothing except there was a conversation. No threats, promises, or intimidation. I wasn't too surprised that the judge denied my motion; judges don't like to take a case from the jury. When they do, it makes the jury feel that their time on the jury was wasted. Judges have to run for election every four years, which means they are politicking for election at every trial. Got to make the jury feel special. But I think I can convince this jury of the failure of the prosecution to prove its case against *any* of us. Even Patel says the information you gave him that night didn't convince him not to testify. And the proof of that is that he showed up on the day of trial—still planning to testify. And Andy, your asking him if he was stupid surely is no crime. I think the jury will see that. So, let's just stick to our plan. We'll have a big celebration when this is over. What do you think?"

"I agree, Jim," said Reid. "We just stick to the plan. Agree, Andy?"

"Agree," replied Andy.

"Both of you will testify this afternoon. That should take us close to 5:00. The judge is unlikely to have us give closings today. She'll send the jury home, and we'll give closings in the morning. That works to our advantage. Our evidence—your testimony—will be the last testimony the jury will hear. They can digest it overnight. Always good to have your best evidence at the end of the day, before the prosecution has an opportunity to rebut it."

When the court reconvened, Judge Feather looked at the defense table and asked, "Mr. Colosimo, do you wish to make an opening statement?"

"Yes, I do," replied Colosimo as he rose and walked toward the jury, stopping about fifteen feet in front of the jurors in the front row.

"Members of the jury. Now that you have heard all the evidence that the prosecutor could present, you should now have one question burning in your minds. And that is, *Just what am I doing here as a juror? Why are these three men facing these charges?* I noted throughout the testimony of Mr. Patel that you were all very attentive. And yet you heard no evidence that anyone made to Mr. Patel any threats of physical force, or intimidation, or promises of benefits of any kind. What the prosecution did show is that Mr. Reid and Mr. McDowell informed Mr. Patel of his rights. How that can be perceived as a crime is beyond imagination. That criminal charges have been made for this lawful conduct should concern you. And it should concern you that you have been called from your work or your home for naught.

"However, if you are not already asking why these charges have been brought, listen carefully to the evidence we will present. We will present the sworn testimony of Mr. Reid and Mr. McDowell, the two men who visited Mr. Patel at his convenience store. They will tell you what really happened that night, that they simply reviewed for him his constitutional and legal rights. He listened. He wanted to know. This action by Mr. Reid and Mr. McDowell was welcomed by Mr. Patel and should be commended by everyone interested in a fair criminal trial.

"Now let me ask a question that you must answer in your mind. Did you hear anything in the evidence presented by the prosecutor that connected me to this crime? Did you even hear my name mentioned? And of course, you did not. Not once! Yet, here I stand, not only as defense counsel but as a defendant. That should be sufficient to add to your concern about why these charges have been brought. So, listen carefully to the testimony of Mr. Reid and Mr. McDowell, who will tell you—under their sworn oath—that I was not involved in any way with their visit to see Mr. Patel. They will confirm that I was not even aware they were going to see Mr. Patel. Their job, as they informed Mr. DeBickero when he questioned them, was to get the case ready for trial. They saw a need to inform a witness of his rights. That was all they intended to do and that is all they did.

"At the end of this trial, after Judge Feather has given her final instructions, I am confident you will do the right thing—bring in a verdict of 'not guilty' for all defendants of all charges. Thank you."

Colosimo called Tom Reid as his first witness. Reid was sworn, took his seat, and introductory questions revealed he was an employee of Colosimo's law firm. There were no questions about his education or background.

"What are your duties at the Colosimo law firm?"

"Most of the cases at our law firm involve criminal defense, so I help in interviewing witnesses, investigating charges, and in various ways getting the case ready for trial. We have cases across the state, and I help with the logistics—preparing exhibits and getting them to the courthouse, arranging for accommodations, and so forth."

"Now, directing your attention to the night of October 5 of last year, do you recall making a visit to a convenience store known as Fast Eddies, here in Savannah?"

"Yes, I do."

"What was the purpose of your visit?"

"I wanted to speak to Mr. Patel, the owner of the store. He was a possible witness in a trial our office was preparing for. I was convinced that his testifying in the trial was not in his best interest. I wanted to inform him of his rights."

"Is Mr. Patel the same Mr. Patel who testified here earlier for the prosecution?"

"Yes."

"Did you meet with him that night?"

"Yes, I did."

"Was anyone else with you at the time?"

"Yes, another associate of our law firm, Anderson McDowell."

"Did anyone direct you to go visit Mr. Patel?"

"No. And no one but Mr. McDowell and I knew we were going. We discussed it, but we didn't tell anyone else we were going. It was our decision alone. We knew it was the right thing to do. Our job is to help get the case ready for trial."

"Are you swearing to this jury that I had nothing to do with your visit and knew nothing about it before you left?"

"Absolutely."

"During your conversation with Mr. Patel, did you threaten his person in any way?"

"Certainly not."

"Threaten his employment in any way?"

"No."

"Did you threaten any other person or any property?"

"We did not."

"Did you offer him any reward or benefit—of any kind?"

"We did not."

"Did you encourage him in any way to change his testimony?"

"We did not."

"Did you encourage him in any way not to testify as a witness?"

"We did not—all we did was advise him of his rights."

"I have no further questions."

"Cross-exam, Mr. Marino?"

"Yes, Your Honor." Scott walked toward the lectern, but stopped, turning to face the witness. He had researched Reid's background for information that he could use for impeachment. He had a conviction for a drug offense, but that would not be admissible, and even though Reid had been disbarred, the acts that led to the disbarment were not admissible under Georgia evidence law. Reid had been disbarred for comingling his client's trust account with his personal account, plus failing to give two clients professional representation. On one occasion, he failed to even appear at trial to represent a client in a criminal case, and on another occasion, he showed up inebriated and was cited for contempt of court. He possibly may have received only a license suspension had he submitted a plan for rehabilitation, but he refused to cooperate with bar counsel, resulting in his disbarment. However, none of these bad acts were admissible in a Georgia criminal trial, so Scott's cross-exam would be limited to his sworn testimony just presented.

"Mr. Reid, you state you visited Mr. Patel because you were convinced that his testifying at the trial was not in his best interest, right?"

"Yes."

"That was the criminal trial of Max Gordon?"

"Yes."

"And your law firm was representing Mr. Gordon?"

"Yes."

"So, the real reason you contacted him was that his testimony would not be in the best interest of your client—Max Gordon. Isn't that correct?"

"No, I thought he was making a mistake. The prosecutor had given him a pretrial agreement he didn't need—all he had to do was not testify, and the charges against him could not be proved."

"But if he did testify, the charges against Max Gordon would likely be proved, right?"

"I have no way of knowing."

"You have no way of knowing? You had discussed that with your boss, Mr. Colosimo, hadn't you?"

"I don't recall such a discussion."

"Had you discussed your belief that his testifying was not in his best interest with his defense counsel?"

"No, I had not."

"You knew he had a defense counsel, didn't you?"

"I assumed he did, but I wasn't certain."

"Did you ask him?"

"No."

"Mr. Reid, you were once a practicing attorney, weren't you?"

"Objection!" Colosimo was now standing. "Irrelevant, prejudicial, and more!"

"More?" Judge Feather looked at Colosimo with a repressed smile on her face. "That is an objection I'm not familiar with."

"Well, surely irrelevant and prejudicial."

"Counsel, please approach the bench."

Once at the bench, Judge Feather turned to Scott. "Mr. Marino, do you have a response to Mr. Colosimo's objections—irrelevant and prejudicial?"

"Your Honor, I have evidence that this witness was once a practicing attorney. As much as I would like to, I am not planning to ask him about his disbarment. However, because of his experience as an attorney, he would know that when a witness is represented by counsel any contact with the witness must be through counsel. This just shows the deliberate deception on the part of this witness in contacting Mr. Patel. His mission was to prevent his testimony. He took advantage of a person under extreme stress and confronted him with false and misleading statements for the purpose of having him not testify. He did not contact Mr. Patel through counsel—in fact, he urged Mr. Patel not to discuss their visit with counsel. That is the relevancy, and if it's prejudicial to the defense case, so be it. 'Prejudicial' is not grounds for exclusion if it is legally relevant."

Judge Feather did not hesitate. "The objections are overruled."

Scott returned to his position in front of the witness. "I ask you once again, you were once a practicing attorney, weren't you?"

"Yes."

"Then surely you are aware that any contact with a witness represented by counsel must be through his counsel, right?"

"I wasn't sure he was represented by counsel."

"So, you asked him?"

There was no response from the witness, who turned his head in the direction of the defense table, expecting another objection. But there was none.

"You knew Mr. Patel was extremely stressed about the charges he was facing, didn't you?"

"I would expect that."

"And you assured him there was a way out, correct?"

"Yes, because there was."

"You told him the way out was because of the 'two-witness rule,' correct?"

"Yes. It was applicable."

"But you did not tell him that 'one witness plus corroborating circumstances' is sufficient to prove perjury, did you?"

"I wasn't aware of that."

"And it didn't matter anyway, did it, because your purpose was to confuse the witness by feeding him misinformation and to have him lose confidence in his attorney, wasn't it?"

"No."

"You wanted him to believe he was being offered up to the prosecution on a platter, didn't you, Mr. Reid? In fact, those were your exact words, weren't they?"

"I don't recall that."

"Of course not. Your recalling that was not important. But you wanted Mr. Patel to recall that, didn't you?"

No response from the witness.

"And you heard him testify this morning to those exact words, didn't you?"

No response.

"I have no further questions."

"Redirect, Mr. Colosimo?"

Colosimo rose and cocked his head for a long moment as if

contemplating an answer. Finally, he responded, "No, we'll call our next witness, Anderson McDowell."

Just as McDowell rose to leave the defense table for the witness box, the lights flickered, then the courtroom went dark. And almost immediately the emergency floodlights came on in the courtroom.

"All please remain seated," said Judge Feather. "The bailiff will check with security to see if this is a very temporary power outage or if we are in for a longer wait."

The bailiff was back in about five minutes and informed Judge Feather that it was a transformer problem. Georgia Power had reported that it would be at least an hour before power was restored, likely more.

Judge Feather addressed the semi-dark courtroom. "We can't be sure when the power will return, so I am recessing court until 9:00 tomorrow morning." She cautioned the jury about listening to the radio or reading the local papers, and the courtroom began to empty.

As Scott was leaving, he heard a familiar voice. "Hi, Scott. Didn't pay your electric bill again?"

Scott turned; it was Bill Baldwin. "No lights needed—justice is blind," said Scott, smiling. "Bill, what brings you out to the courthouse on such a beautiful spring day. Must be another slow news day."

"Well, it's not the trial of the century, but when a hot-shot Atlanta criminal defense lawyer is on trial, representing himself plus two co-defendants, it makes for a very interesting story. The *National Law Journal* thinks so too. They sent Roger Curlin—remember him? He covered the Harrison trials."

"Of course, I remember Roger. Really good reporter. I saved his articles on the Harrison trials."

"And you saved mine, too. Right?"

"Of course, Bill. Got a basement full of 'em." They both laughed.

"Now that you have the afternoon off and no electricity to play video games in your office, how about joining me for a drink?"

Scott stopped and thought for a moment. "Yes, I'm for that. How about making it at the Library? Jennifer has a seminar at Savannah Law on Tuesdays. Maybe I can get her on the phone, and she can meet us there."

"Good. I'll see you there about 5:00."

CHAPTER THIRTY-EIGHT
Tuesday, April 21

Scott and Bill arrived at the same time and entered the Library together. They saw Juri serving a couple of customers at the end of the bar. Juri saw the two entering, and a smile immediately flashed across his face. By the time they had taken their seats at the bar, two frozen mugs of beer were sliding down the bar top, stopping right in front of his two new guests.

"Perfect!" Juri proclaimed in a loud voice. But his broad smile faded as he walked toward them. There was disappointment on his face, and Scott knew the source: the Atlanta Braves. They had lost to the Washington Nationals Monday night by one run.

"So, you watched the game last night, right?" asked Scott as he picked up his beer in both hands, smiling.

"I did. Watched them lose to the lousy Nationals. If they can't beat the Nationals, they are done. Seems they can't beat anybody. Lost six of their last seven games."

Scott was not aware of that, but he knew the Braves had stumbled recently, and he didn't question Juri when it came to the Braves' record. He was a walking encyclopedia of Braves' statistics and facts.

"Season is early, Juri. I recall being here the day after they won two in a row to open the season. You predicted that this was their year."

"Shows you how much I know." He shook his head slowly for a long moment, and then a smile returned to his face.

"I've got a couple of good ones. Want a lawyer story or a reporter story?"

"Lawyer," Bill quickly responded.

"Looks like Bill scooped you, Scott. Lawyer jokes are more fun anyway. And easy—about everything they do is a joke."

"Enough Juri. Next time you get sued by some drunk who fell off a bar stool and busted his head, call a reporter to defend you."

"I'll think about it. But here's a good one."

Juri took his usual stance for one of his "stories." He stood erect, with shoulders braced, then took a step back.

"This lawyer telephones the governor. It's just after midnight and the governor's aide answers. Lawyer says 'I need to talk to the governor regarding a really urgent matter.'

"Aide says, 'The governor is sleeping.'

"'But this is really an urgent matter,' lawyer says. Aide eventually agrees to wake up the governor.

"Governor wakes up, picks up the phone, grumbling. 'So, what is it?'

"'Judge Stark has just died,' lawyer says, 'and I want to take his place.'" Juri now takes a step forward and begins to smile, looking from Bill to Scott and back to Bill.

"'Well, it's OK with me if it's OK with the undertaker,' governor says and hangs up."

Juri starts the laughter and is soon joined in by his captive audience. And as usual, his audience rated the joke, thumbs down. Still, the laughter was genuine. A couple of customers came and sat at the bar, and Juri walked over to serve them.

"So, lawyer jokes aside, how's the trial going from the prosecutor's view?" asked Bill.

"Not sure. Our witnesses came through as expected, and so did Colosimo's witness. I think we have a good shot at convicting his two stooges but haven't been able to connect Colosimo directly. Not sure a jury will be as certain as I am that Colosimo directed the visit to Patel. It's a circumstantial case—we just hope we have a jury intelligent enough to know that two office employees of a one-attorney defense firm would not travel from Atlanta to Savannah—250 miles—and engage in a conversation with a witness without their boss directing them to do it. But that's what we are relying on. How do you look at it?"

"About the same. Looks like they are willing to take the rap for their boss. Must be a big payoff. But if my reading on this trial is correct, you prefer to get the lawyer rather than his two stooges, as you call them. Right?"

"Right. He's the main actor for corruption in this case. And of course, we would like to put a corrupt attorney out of business. Locking up his two employees won't do that. You heard Juri. Lawyer jokes are easy, he says—and lawyers like Colosimo make it easy."

"How many additional witnesses do you expect the defense to present?"

"Well, they have the younger guy—McDowell—who was about to take the stand this afternoon, when the lights went out. He's for sure. Don't know if 'Diamond Jim' will testify, but I hope he does."

"Why?"

"Because most defendants—especially guilty defendants—who testify, do their case more harm than good. I think I'll have a better shot at connecting him to the visit if he testifies. He can't add anything to help the defense case, so he won't testify. Colosimo is a corrupt attorney, but he's also an experienced and smart trial lawyer. The only thing that may prompt him to testify is his ego."

"Then there's a good chance he'll testify if I read him correctly. He does appear to have an over-sized ego and sense of importance. That diamond-studded wardrobe is a giveaway. We'll know tomorrow." Bill saw that Scott's beer mug was empty.

"Ready for a refill?"

"No. I couldn't get Jennifer on the phone so she's not stopping by. I'll head home and work on my closing. Big day tomorrow."

CHAPTER THIRTY-NINE

Tuesday, April 21

At the same time, Scott and Bill were at the Library, enjoying their beer and discussing the trial, Jessica was back at the Hyatt Regency getting ready for her night out with Andy. She was pleased that this would be their last. She reflected back on her assignment from Colosimo—to keep Andy on track for his testimony. She was quite satisfied with her success in this task as well as her reward: admission to Adam Lansky Law School and tuition paid by Colosimo. She could have her degree by the end of the year.

She had spoken in private with Colosimo soon after they returned to the Hyatt from the courthouse. She assured him that Andy was fully committed to "the plan," but he asked that she text him a report at the end of the night. He confessed that he was a "worrier" and would sleep better knowing all was well. She promised him she would.

Jessica knew just the place for this last night of her assignment: El Escapade, just off Abercorn Street near Oglethorpe Mall. She had been there several times while at Savannah Law and it was her favorite Latin dance club in Savannah. It had an extensive menu and a large dance floor. Although there was rarely a live band, the DJ was very good and had an extensive selection of popular Latin songs—the perfect place to celebrate her final night with Andy.

They left the Hyatt a little after 7:00 with Jessica driving her car. She knew the streets quite well, and after a twenty-minute leisurely drive, arrived at El Escapade. Even though it was a Tuesday night, there was a large crowd, and the DJ was playing a familiar Latin song that they could hear as she parked her car in the restaurant's lot. She opened her door, turned and looked at Andy, and said, "Let's go! This is going to be a fun night!" Andy grinned broadly and followed her into the El Escapade.

It was as Jessica had proclaimed, a fun night. They ordered drinks and dinner and joined in the dancing to Latin music. Andy had become reasonably proficient in a few of the Latin dances, and they were often on the dance floor. When seated, Jessica turned the conversation into their plans to study at Adam Lansky and hopefully one day open up their own law firm. Jessica alluded twice to their planned rendezvous in her room at the Hyatt, earning a broad smile from Andy each time.

As they were preparing to leave and Andy was paying the bill, Jessica excused herself to visit the ladies' room. A few minutes prior, she had received a call from her aunt in Atlanta and had placed the phone on the table beside her. During her absence, the phone beeped. Andy saw that it was a text message. He picked up the phone and read.

> "I'm tired—turning in.
> No need to text unless
> Andy weakens re plan."

Andy weakens re plan? What could that mean? wondered Andy. He saw that the text was just the latest text in a chain of text messages. He moved up the chain to the next text message—one sent from Jessica's phone.

> "Out with Andy tonight. No
> changes. He's still happy

just rounding the bases
with my promise of a home
run at the Hyatt after
the trial. (No way!).”

He moved up the text chain and read an incoming message. He did
not recognize the phone number, but it gave him a good clue to the
owner of the phone.

“Keep him committed.
Spoke with dean at Adam
Lansky. No need to worry
about being admitted.”

Andy continued his examination of the messages, the next one sent
from Jessica’s phone.

“Date with Andy tonight.
No talk about the trial.
He seems committed to the deal.
Still running the bases!”

The next text was an incoming message. Andy still did not recognize
the phone number of the sender, but he was now sure of who was
sending the texts.

“Good work. I’m counting
on you to keep him committed
to the plan.”

Andy quickly read all the text messages in the chain, then placed the
phone down in the original position where Jessica had laid it. He was
stunned—and sickened—by the revelation it had given him. *Couldn’t
be*, he thought. *Is this some planned joke? This can’t be real.* But as much

as he wished it not to be real, he knew that indeed it was. How could he have been so taken in by this beautiful young lady? He was embarrassed by his naivety. Slowly his shock was turning to anger. He had to be careful to keep his emotions under control.

Jessica returned to the table. Andy stood and said, "I've paid the bill; we can leave now." Jessica smiled, picked up her phone, and they walked to her car.

Jessica did most of the talking on the ride back to the Hyatt. Andy answered her questions but otherwise contributed little to the conversation. "Andy, you have been so quiet. Is something wrong?" Jessica asked as they neared the hotel.

"Oh, I'm OK, just looking forward to tomorrow," Andy responded, faking a broad smile.

"Me, too," Jessica responded, returning the smile.

CHAPTER FORTY

Wednesday, April 22

The court was called to order shortly after 9:00 a.m. The three defendants were seated in their usual positions, Colosimo in the middle. Judge Feather looked at the defense table. "Call your next witness, Mr. Colosimo."

"We call Anderson McDowell." McDowell rose from his seat, walked to the witness stand and was sworn in.

"Mr. McDowell, would you please give the jury your full name and your occupation."

"My name is Anderson H. McDowell, and I work as a paralegal and investigator for the Colosimo Law Firm."

"That is my law firm, correct?"

"Yes."

"How long have you worked for my law firm?"

"Three and a half years."

"What is your education?"

"I have an undergraduate degree in Business Administration and a JD degree from Clarence Darrow Law School in Nashville."

"Are you a member of any state bar?"

"Not yet, but I hope to be."

"While in law school, did you receive instructions in ethics and professional conduct?"

"Yes, we had a course—Professional Responsibility—which was required of all students."

"May we assume you did quite well in that course, Mr. McDowell?" Colosimo chuckled and smiled broadly at the jury.

"I did."

"From that course and from the instructions and experience you received while employed by my law firm, have you learned appropriate and ethical practices when interviewing trial witnesses?"

"I have."

"Did you interview a witness by the name of Vijay Patel last October?"

"Yes, I did."

"Where did that interview take place?"

"Here in Savannah at his convenience store on Waters Avenue."

"Who besides yourself and Mr. Patel were present?"

"Thomas Reid, who testified here yesterday."

"I want you to turn to the jury and tell them all about that visit. What was said—start from the beginning and tell how the visit originated."

"The visit originated when you called Mr. Reid and me into your office and instructed us to pay a visit to Mr. Patel. That was . . ."

Colosimo extended his palm out toward McDowell, and loudly said, "Stop!"

McDowell became silent.

Colosimo turned to Judge Feather. "May we have a short recess?"

"It's a bit early for a recess, Mr. Colosimo. We have just started this session."

"Then may I have a moment to consult?" responded Colosimo.

"Consult with whom, Mr. Colosimo? You do not have a cocounsel."

Colosimo looked perplexed. And he was. This was not the testimony he expected. Jessica has assured him McDowell was still committed to the plan. Yet, what McDowell had just said indicated "the plan" was about to go off the rails. Colosimo was an experienced trial lawyer and had had his share of witnesses testify to something unexpected. But this was a codefendant—and his client—who now was apparently about to implicate him into the alleged crime. This was directly contrary to the plan they had worked out. Was it about to be unraveled, or had McDowell merely misspoke? He looked into the packed gallery and saw Jessica, her face tense, a frightened look.

"Just a quick consultation with an employee of my law firm."

"I'll give you a moment, Mr. Colosimo. Make it short."

Colosimo motioned Jessica to come forward. Jessica met him at the bar that separated the gallery. Colosimo whispered. *"Did you hear what Andy said? What the hell is going on with him? You assured me he was still committed to the plan."*

Jessica whispered back, *"He was committed as of last night. Maybe he just misspoke."*

Colosimo whispered, *"I'm going to dismiss him; we'll just rely on Tom's testimony."* He turned and walked toward the bench, and Jessica returned to her seat.

"We have no further questions, the witness is excused," said Colosimo.

"He's not excused yet, Mr. Colosimo. The State may wish to cross-examine."

"And I do wish to cross-examine," said Scott, as he rose from his seat at the prosecution table. Scott realized he was taking a chance examining McDowell, as he did not know how he would respond. He was quite aware of the established rule to not ask a question of a witness when you don't know the answer. But his instinct told him that his cross-examination would reveal some very probative evidence for the prosecution.

"Mr. McDowell, your attorney asked you to turn to the jury and tell them all about your visit to Savannah to interview Mr. Patel. He asked that you start at the beginning. And you said you were called into Mr. Colosimo's office and given instructions to visit Mr. Patel. At that time, Mr. Colosimo held up his hand and asked you to stop your testimony. Now, I want you to tell the jury what Mr. Colosimo told you when he called you into his office."

Colosimo was immediately on his feet. "Objection! Calls for hearsay!"

Judge Feather looked at Colosimo disapprovingly. This was a foolish objection to clearly admissible evidence, and she was sure Colosimo knew that it was foolish. Judge Feather surmised the objection was made out of desperation.

"Overruled."

"Go ahead, Mr. McDowell," said Scott, "tell the jury what Mr. Colosimo told you when he called you into his office."

"We were told to visit Mr. Patel in Savannah. He suggested the time and date—late Monday when there would be few customers, and we would have a better opportunity to speak with him alone."

"Did he tell you the purpose of your visit?"

"Yes. We were to convince Mr. Patel that it was not in his best interest to testify. We knew he would be testifying with a pretrial agreement. Our job was to convince him that this would be a mistake."

"Did he give you any suggestions on how to accomplish this?"

McDowell paused a long moment before responding. He knew he was not only implicating his boss, but he was incriminating himself as well. But the disappointment and the anger that he had experienced the previous night were driving him. He would be sentenced to prison but so would Colosimo who had directed this activity. His only regret was that the cunning and devious young lady who had led him on for the past six weeks would escape unscathed.

"He instructed us not to make any threats to him as this would likely cause him to contact law enforcement or his lawyer. We were to suggest his lawyer was not leveling with him and that by testifying his lawyer was just serving him up to the prosecution. Over the next few days, we had several sessions where Mr. Colosimo discussed how best to accomplish what we were trying to do—especially how to keep Mr. Patel's lawyer out of it. A major part of the plan was to assure Mr. Patel that he had a sure defense to the perjury charges he was facing because of 'the two-witness rule.' Tom was to lead the interview. I think Mr. Colosimo had more confidence in Tom Reid than he did in me—Tom had been with him longer and had more experience."

"Mr. McDowell, you were called as a witness for the defense, but considering the testimony you have just given, I want you to tell the jury if you are testifying under a pretrial agreement, or if you have been contacted in any way by me or any member of the District Attorney's office concerning your testimony."

"No, I have not. My testimony is a result of a decision I made on my own, and I'm aware of the consequences of my testimony."

"I have no further questions."

"Mr. Colosimo, do you wish to redirect?"

Colosimo had been considering this question during the entire cross-examination. Were there any questions he could ask on redirect to counter this disastrous testimony by this defector? He could think of none. Further examination of this witness would likely just dig a deeper hole for the defense. He would have to find a way in his closing argument to account for this "false" testimony.

"I have no redirect."

"Mr. McDowell, you may take your seat back at the defense table," said Judge Feather.

Usually, witnesses were excused after testifying—free to leave the courtroom. But this witness was a defendant and would have to remain. McDowell returned to his seat on the left of Colosimo. Their eyes did not meet. It was a tense moment. As he was about to take his seat, McDowell quickly jerked his chair about a foot farther from Colosimo's. It was obviously meant to visually display his contempt for his boss. And all the eyes of the jury were on it.

Colosimo knew the next words from Judge Feather would be for him to call his next witness. He had intended to have only the two witnesses: Reid and McDowell. He had made no plans to testify and subject himself to cross-examination. Now, after hearing McDowell's unexpected testimony, he had to reconsider.

The expected words came. "Call your next witness, Mr. Colosimo."

"May I have a moment?"

"Briefly, yes."

Years of experience had taught him that he should never have a witness testify without proper preparation. He quickly decided that applied to him. He had not given any thoughts to testifying in this trial. For the first time in his many years as a trial lawyer, he was frozen in thought. And frightened. He made a quick decision.

CHAPTER FORTY-ONE

Wednesday, April 22

"The defense rests."

Scott was surprised. He had not expected Colosimo to testify, but after McDowell's shocking testimony, he did not see how he could avoid taking the stand to refute it. His failure to testify now was as unexpected as McDowell's testimony.

"Does the prosecution have a case in rebuttal?" asked Judge Feather.

"No, Your Honor."

The judge turned to the jury. "I have some important matters to take up with counsel. Bailiff, please escort the jury to the jury room."

The "important matters" were the jury instructions she would be giving the jury before their deliberations. Counsel would hear the instructions the judge planned to give and would have an opportunity to object or propose additional instructions. There were only two charges against each of the defendants. There were no major objections or proposed additional instructions by either counsel, and the session on instructions was quickly over.

"We will take a twenty-minute recess, then hear closing arguments," said Judge Feather.

After McDowell's testimony, Scott began thinking about how his previously prepared closing argument would have to change. Twenty minutes seemed by far too little time for a rewrite, but the limited time also applied to the defense, and Colosimo had a much harder revision to undertake. Scott and Fasi began to confer, but the twenty minutes expired before much was accomplished. Scott would have to wing it.

The court was called to order and the jury was in place. "The prosecution may make its closing argument," said Judge Feather.

Scott rose and walked toward the jury, stopping in front and center of the first row. "May it please the court, and members of the jury," Scott began. "In my opening statement at the beginning of this trial, I stood here and said that this would not be a long trial and would not be a difficult case. We would prove the charges with only four prosecution witnesses. As it turned out, we had five prosecution witnesses, one we did not expect, Anderson McDowell. And one we did not need, as you had all the evidence necessary in this case before Mr. McDowell was called as a witness. So, let's just call Mr. McDowell the 'bonus witness.'

"Each of the defendants is charged with the same two crimes— influencing witnesses and conspiracy to influence witnesses. Before you retire to the jury room to deliberate, Judge Feather will explain the elements of those crimes—that is, the facts that the prosecution must have proved beyond a reasonable doubt in order to find any defendant guilty. You will learn that for a conviction of influencing witnesses, threats, or offers of some reward, are not required. It is sufficient if the defendant engaged in misleading conduct toward another person with the intent to influence, delay, or prevent the testimony of any person in an official proceeding. And you heard proof of that from Mr. Patel.

"The two night-time visitors misled Mr. Patel by falsely suggesting there was a way out of the charges against him. They suggested that his attorney was working with the prosecutor, that perhaps money had changed hands or that his attorney needed a favor from the prosecutor for someone else his attorney was defending. They suggested he look up the two-witness rule on the Internet, knowing it would confuse him and give credence to their suggestion that his attorney was not working for him. They led him to have such doubts in his attorney that he was afraid to even speak with his attorney about their visit. They suggested that his attorney was 'serving him up on a platter to the prosecutor as a sacrificial lamb'—their words. And one of these night-time visitors was at the courthouse to greet him—just in case he didn't get their message the first time. The combination of their actions was just as they had planned and hoped for; he did not testify against Mr. Colosimo's client and the client was acquitted.

"Although the complicity of Mr. Colosimo in the crimes was not specifically mentioned in Mr. Patel's testimony, there should be no doubt that those two employees of Mr. Colosimo did not travel to Savannah and engage in that conversation with Mr. Patel without the specific encouragement and direction of their boss and codefendant, James Colosimo. But now that you have heard from the 'bonus witness,' you have direct evidence of that."

Scott proceeded to outline the elements of proof for the second offense charged—conspiracy—explaining that it consisted of conspiring with one or more and an overt act. "Can there be any reasonable doubt based on the evidence you have heard, that there was a conspiracy between these three defendants to influence a witness—Mr. Patel—to not testify?

"I am not aware of why Mr. McDowell took the witness stand today to confess to his crimes and the circumstances surrounding them. That defendant took the stand of his own volition and in his own words swore to tell the truth, 'so help me God.' You should consider his testimony along with all the other evidence in the case.

"I want to thank you for serving on this jury. You have listened carefully to the evidence. You will soon have an opportunity to complete the final duty that comes with your responsibility as a juror—to render a verdict. After you deliberate and consider the evidence, I am confident that you will return a verdict that speaks the truth, a verdict as to each charge and against each defendant that is consistent with your oath as a juror, a verdict of guilty."

Scott returned to the prosecution table and took his seat. Fasi gave him a nod and a smile. Colosimo stood and walked to the lectern.

"Mr. Marino has asked that you render a verdict that 'speaks the truth.' We ask the same. The evidence shows you that two men visited a witness and explained his rights. His rights under the law of this land—the right not to testify. The District Attorney—for whatever reason you may imagine—has determined that in his Alice and Wonderland, this is a crime. How original—and how wrong. Yes, we want a verdict that 'speaks the truth,' and we want a verdict that informs the District Attorney that his job is to enforce the law, not to *make* the law.

"Let's now examine the real facts in this case. Mr. McDowell and Mr. Reid advised Mr. Patel that he should follow a three-part plan. First, not to be a sacrificial lamb. That's a crime? Apparently, the prosecution thinks so.

"Second, it was suggested that Mr. Patel check into the 'two-witness rule' that would provide a defense to the charges of perjury that he was facing. Mr. Schaub, his defense counsel, testified that proof of perjury requires two witnesses or one witness plus corroborating circumstances. And he says he did not pursue this defense—or even inform his client of this defense—because there were corroborating circumstances. But did you hear any of those corroborating *circumstances*? That is a plural word—but did you hear *even one* corroborating circumstance? You did not.

"The third suggestion was to consider carefully whether to discuss their visit with his attorney. Note Mr. Patel said they did not tell him not to discuss their visit, but to just consider it carefully. Perhaps that's a crime in China, but by your verdict, you can tell the DA that's not a crime in the USA.

"Now, let me address the bizarre testimony of Mr. McDowell. I'm sure this was as big a surprise to you as it was to me. I've been trying cases for over thirty years and never encountered such a scene as this witness presented. At first, I thought perhaps he was having a psychiatric breakdown. What could possess him to testify to such falsehood and deliberate lies? And then it came to me when Mr. Marino asked him if he was testifying under a pretrial agreement or if anyone from the DA's office had contacted him. I was slow on the pickup, but then it became obvious. This witness was bought by the prosecutor—hook, line, and sinker. The total works. This lying turncoat witness was indeed testifying under a secret agreement."

Scott was on his feet. "Objection! There is no evidence to support that statement!"

"Sustained. The jury will disregard that statement by Mr. Colosimo." Judge Feather looked sternly at Colosimo and then said, "Counsel please approach the bench."

As soon as counsel were assembled at the bench, Judge Feather faced Colosimo and spoke through tightened lips. "No more of that Mr. Colosimo. And don't test me." She sat back in her chair, and counsel returned to their previous positions.

Colosimo quickly wrapped up his closing with the usual emphasis on the burden of proof and reasonable doubt. But his words were hollow and his voice lacked vitality, portraying a heavy doubt in his own words. He paused, his head lowered with his eyes on the floor in front of him, before facing the jury and quietly saying, "thanks." His thirty years of trying cases was not evident. He turned and walked slowly back to the defense table.

Even before he was seated, Judge Feather looked at the prosecution table and said, "Mr. Marino, you may make the final closing."

"May I have just a moment, Your Honor?"

"Yes; make it brief."

Scott had been considering what he could say that would be more persuasive for his case than what had just taken place in front of the jury. He had never prosecuted a case in which he had forgone the opportunity to make a final closing argument. In fact, he had never heard of a case in which the prosecutor gave up the opportunity to have the final word. He quickly conferred with his co-counsel, then made his decision.

"We have nothing further, Your Honor."

Judge Feather then gave the jury their final instructions, and the jury retired to the jury room to begin their deliberations. The "waiting"—the most stressful time for defendants, defense counsel, and prosecutors—would now begin.

Two hours later, there was a knock on the door, and the foreperson informed the bailiff waiting outside, "We have a verdict."

Scott had returned to his office to wait when his phone rang informing him there was a verdict. He looked at his watch. Two hours was a short deliberation, giving concern to Scott. He had heard the legal lore that a short deliberation usually means a defense verdict and a long deliberation suggests a guilty verdict. But he had also heard that was merely a myth. This trial was a very short criminal trial—only two trial days after jury selection. There wasn't a lot of testimony for the jury to consider. He returned immediately to the courtroom. He would soon know.

CHAPTER FORTY-TWO

Wednesday, April 22

The gallery of the courtroom was rapidly filling with spectators as Scott and Fasi entered and took their seats at the prosecution table. Only McDowell was seated at the defense table. Scott gazed into the gallery and saw Colosimo, Reid, and Jessica standing and talking. Colosimo and Reid made no effort to move to the defense table until a bailiff approached them and directed that they take their seats. McDowell saw them walking toward the defense table and he quickly and forcefully moved his chair another foot to the side away from his boss, a visual act of defiance to his boss.

Judge Feather entered, called the court to order and directed that the bailiff bring the jury into the courtroom. The jury was soon seated in the jury box, and the courtroom became very quiet. The judge looked at the jury.

"Has the jury reached a verdict?"

A tall man of about sixty rose with the verdict forms in his hand. "We have."

The judge directed the bailiff to take the forms and bring them to the bench. She read them, handed them to the clerk to be published, and directed that the three defendants stand.

The verdict for Colosimo came first. The clerk read each count. And to each of the two counts in the indictment, she pronounced the findings in her strong voice.

"Guilty . . . Guilty."

The verdict for Thomas Reid was next. Reid folded his arms, lowered his head, and kept his eyes focused on the floor before him.

"Guilty . . . Guilty."

The final verdict was for Anderson McDowell. He looked directly at the clerk as she announced the verdict on the two counts.

"Not Guilty . . . Not Guilty."

The silent courtroom immediately transformed into a gaggle of voices. Scott looked at Fasi with astonishment. Moments later, Judge Feather gave a sharp rap with her gavel. Her signal quieted the gallery quickly. She then polled the jury. Each juror confirmed that this was his or her verdict.

"Mr. Colosimo and Mr. Reid are remanded to the sheriff of Chatham County to await sentencing," Judge Feather said. "Sentencing is set for May 11. I am requesting an expedited presentence investigation. Mr. McDowell, you are free to go." She then thanked the jury for their service and adjourned the court as bailiffs took Colosimo and Reid into custody.

Scott stood, placed some papers in his briefcase, and faced his cocounsel. "Not guilty verdict for the only defendant that admitted he was guilty?" Scott shook his head from side to side. "What do you make of that, Joe?"

"Just another form of jury nullification. It has a long history. It was especially popular during prohibition, when juries often would not convict because they opposed the law. But I don't think this jury's verdict was because they opposed the law. I think it was just a 'thank you' to McDowell. He made their decision easier. Without it, they would have no direct evidence to connect Colosimo, and some on the jury would have a difficult time convicting him, even though they 'believed' him guilty. But beyond a reasonable doubt? Maybe not. But with McDowell's testimony, they had that direct testimony. They knew McDowell was guilty—he confessed—but less guilty than Reid, the more experienced associate and certainly less guilty than Colosimo. So, they just gave him that 'not guilty' verdict in appreciation of his testimony that saved them that difficult choice. It's the beauty of the jury system. We have to learn not to question it. Twelve minds in the jury box may be better at dispensing justice than the mind of a lone judge on the bench."

Scott and Fasi picked up their briefcases and followed the spectators out of the courtroom to return to their offices. There were many case files on their desks needing attention. For prosecutors, winning a trial did not mean a financial reward as it did in civil practice. Yet, the quiet satisfaction in the results of one such as this—a corrupt attorney identified and removed—provided reward enough.

As the courtroom emptied, two individuals who had played important roles in the results were in a conversation near the jury box. It was Jessica and McDowell.

"Now that the trial is over, maybe you can tell me just why you broke from the plan," said Jessica. "You gave up a great opportunity and job in Jim's law firm. We both could be starting law school at Adam Lansky this summer. So now that the law firm is disbanded, what do you plan to be doing?"

"Long term, I'm not sure. Short term, I plan to stay in Savannah a few days—a vacation. I like the city. Visit some of the sights, some of the night clubs. Sit on the benches in Forsyth Park and gaze at the fountain. Maybe join in one of the pickup baseball games like I saw there last Sunday. It seemed to be a friendly group."

"A pickup baseball game?" Jessica said, as a frown appeared on her face.

"Yes. I enjoy the game, especially *rounding the bases. Making it to first base, second base, third, and maybe even making it to home plate*," McDowell said with a broad smile.

Without responding, Jessica stared intently at McDowell for a long moment, her frown turning into a fierce scowl. "You are such a loser," she said, as she turned and walked away.

His response of "rounding the bases" and "making it to home plate" had surprised and quickly upset her. *"How did he know of her part in "the plan"?* It was just too much on point to be coincidental.

He apparently had become fully aware of the "agreement." She tried to dismiss it, but it played on her mind. She went to the Hyatt, checked out, and was soon in her car on her way back to Atlanta.

The "rounding the bases" comment was soon replaced with thoughts of what she would be doing now that her "assignment" was over. Foremost in her mind was completing that final semester at Adam Lansky. She knew she would not be attending with her tuition and books paid by Colosimo—plus a $2,000 monthly maintenance check—as promised in the "contract." It was unenforceable from the beginning, but even had it been enforceable, she did not keep her end of the bargain. But that would not affect her admission to Adam Lansky, as Colosimo had already taken care of that. She was confident that her aunt would fund her tuition for this last semester. She could continue working in her aunt's real estate office until finishing law school. Then, she would open her own law office or join one of the law firms in downtown Atlanta. Or perhaps, her graduation from law school would heal the breach with her father, and he would welcome her into his prominent Miami firm. She thought that quite possible, and it would be her first choice.

She stopped in Macon for dinner. McDowell's baseball comment still popped into her mind occasionally. She tried to dismiss it, but still, she wondered. While waiting for her meal in Macon, she called her aunt to tell her that she was on her way home and would be there in about two hours. Her aunt sounded pleased to hear from her and cheerfully reported she had some mail waiting—one piece from Adam Lansky Law School—and the baseball comments by McDowell disappeared from her mind. Her thoughts now turned entirely to graduation from law school and her career ahead.

She parked in her aunt's driveway, grabbed her suitcase and purse, and hurriedly entered the house. Her aunt was apparently upstairs, but she spotted her mail on a nearby table. She quickly sought the one from Adam Lansky and opened it.

Dear Miss Valdez:

We have received your application for admission to Adam Lansky Law School. After carefully considering your application and the accompanying transcript from Savannah College of Law, we regret to inform you that your application has been denied.

Sincerely,
Kim Wilhite
Director of Admission

THE END